Top Secret Identity

Sharon Dunn

Special thanks and acknowledgment to
Sharon Dunn for her contribution
to the Witness Protection miniseries.

Recycling programs for this product may not exist in your area.

™ LOVE INSPIRED BOOKS

ISBN-13: 978-0-373-67601-9

TOP SECRET IDENTITY

www.Harlequin.com

Printed in U.S.A.

Place me like a seal over your heart, like a seal on your arm; for love is as strong as death, its jealousy as unyielding as the grave. It burns like blazing fire, like a mighty flame.

—*Song of Songs* 8:6

For my husband, Michael,
because your support and unconditional love
has made all the difference in the world

ONE

A wave of terror washed over Morgan Smith when she heard the tapping at her window. She gripped the book she'd been reading a little tighter. Someone was outside the caretaker's cottage. Had the man who had tried to kill her in Mexico found her in Iowa?

Though she'd been in witness protection for two months, her fear of being killed had not subsided. Only a few days ago, she'd left Des Moines for the countryside and a job at a stable because she'd felt exposed in the city, vulnerable. She'd grown up on a ranch in Wyoming, and when she worked as an American missionary in Mexico, she'd always chosen to be in rural areas. Wide open spaces felt safer to her.

With her heart pounding, she rose to her feet and walked the short distance to the window, half expecting to see a face contorted with rage or clawlike hands reaching for her neck. The memory of nearly being strangled made her shudder. She stepped closer to the window, where there was only blackness. Yet the sound of the tapping had been too distinct to dismiss as the wind rattling the glass.

A chill snaked down her spine.

Someone was outside.

If the man from Mexico had come to kill her, it seemed odd that he would give her a warning by tapping on the window.

She thought to call her new boss, who was in the guesthouse less than a hundred yards away. Alex Reardon seemed like a nice man. She'd hated being evasive when he'd asked her where she had gotten her knowledge of horses. She'd been fortunate to get the job without references. Her references, everything and everyone she knew—all of that had been stripped from her, even her name. She was no longer Magdalena Chavez. Her new name was Morgan Smith.

The tapping came again, this time at a different window. She whirled around. Paralyzed by terror, she couldn't bring herself to take a step. Did he intend to torment her before he moved in for the kill? With the description she gave them, the U.S. Marshals had tracked down a name for the man who had tried to kill her—Josef Flores, a mercenary for hire, a muscular man known for wearing white suits and killing his victims with his bare hands. But they hadn't caught him yet.

Her pulse drummed in her ears as silence pressed on her from all sides. It had taken her weeks to get out of Mexico alive. Twice, Josef had found her and tried to strangle her. She could still see his bloodshot eyes as he vowed to kill her.

The trouble had started when she became suspicious of some of the practices at the agency where she assisted with international adoptions. Babies were being escorted into the States, instead of adoptive parents coming to Mexico to pick up their children. The behavior of some of the birth mothers was peculiar. At first, they would decide against adoption. Then they would return, days later, saying they'd changed their minds. The young mothers seemed afraid at that second visit. She'd just begun to look through old records and try to contact the mothers when Josef had come after her in her office late at night.

The marshals had agreed to provide her with protection and a new identity because they thought her case might be connected to a larger kidnapping and illegal adoption ring.

Now she stared at the dark window and took in a raspy breath. If what had happened to her was connected to a larger crime, it wouldn't only be Josef who came after her. There could be others.

The knob on the locked door turned and rattled.

She'd been a fool to think the U.S. Marshals could keep her safe.

Clutching her book tighter to her chest, she waited for the moment when the attacker would break down the door and come after her. Morgan steeled herself against the rising panic. She wasn't going to give up that easily. She grabbed her phone to dial 911 but couldn't get a signal in the cottage. She glanced around the room for possible weapons and hiding places.

The door stopped shaking. She waited for a few minutes, tiptoed across the floor and then peeked out the window.

A motion-sensitive light came on in the distance by the stable. She recognized the broad shoulders and denim jacket of Alex Reardon.

What if her would-be attackers hurt Alex? She couldn't let that happen.

Pushing her fear aside, she wrapped her hand around the doorknob, turned it and raced outside. Her feet pounded across the hard-packed dirt toward the stable. She was out of breath by the time she caught up with Alex.

"Alex, what are you doing out so late?"

"I thought I saw somebody run toward the stable." His wavy brown hair appeared soft in the moonlight. "I need to check it out."

"I know—they tapped on my window and shook my door handle. Maybe we should call the police." Fear resonated through each word she uttered.

"Call the police?" He hesitated, probably wondering why she was so panicked. "Why would we do that? My guess is it's just some teenagers messing around. It's happened before. Nothing we can't handle on our own."

Impulsively, she grabbed his upper arm. "I'll go with you then." If something happened to him at her expense, she would never forgive herself.

"All right." Alex shone the flashlight in her direction. "Are you okay to take the inside of the stables? I'll search around the perimeter. We'll meet at the other end." His voice filled with concern.

"I suppose that would be best..." She let go of his arm. "To split up."

His gaze rested on her long enough for her to feel uncomfortable. He probably thought she was flighty, which was not the impression she wanted to give. If only she could explain to him why she was reacting this way. "We could stay together if you want."

"No, we'll go with your plan." Her voice held an intensity that seemed out of place.

He shook his head, clearly confused by her heightened emotions. "Morgan, we live in a really safe part of the country. In all the time that I've lived here, the worst it's ever been was just some bored teenagers looking for something to do." The compassion she heard in his voice helped her let go of some of her fear. "If you do get scared, I won't be far away."

"Okay, I'll search the inside of the stable," she said feeling a little more at ease.

He gave her a reassuring pat on the shoulder and disappeared around the side of the stable.

Morgan stepped into the stable. The door had not been locked, a responsibility that probably fell to her. She was still learning all her duties. She clicked on the lights. By design, the lighting was minimal and subdued to keep the horses calm. She'd need the flashlight to search the dark corners of the barn. She flung open the equipment box and retrieved it. Several of the horses were standing, and the stomping of their hooves and their jerking heads indicated they'd been disturbed by something or someone.

Morgan paced through the long narrow building shining the light where shadows fell. Most of the horses had calmed down except for Bluebell, a black Arabian. Once at the other end of the stable, Morgan pushed open the barn door and stepped out, shining the light in all directions. No Alex. Her heart skipped a beat.

Her voice cracked when she called for him. He was innocent in all this. It wasn't right that he should be hurt in any way. Maybe she had been foolish to move out here, to think she could build some kind of life with this threat hanging over her. The last thing she wanted was someone to get hurt because of the danger she faced.

She heard footsteps and turned just as a body barreled into her. She saw a flash of a plaid material right before she was pushed to the ground. She lay on her back with the wind knocked out of her. Terror raged through her as memories from the attack in Mexico flooded her mind.

Alex called her name from a distance. Her assailant let go of her and retreated into the darkness, probably scared away by Alex's voice.

Alex came around the corner and fell to his knees when he saw her on the ground. His voice filled with concern. "Hey, what happened?"

Morgan blinked. Pain shot through her back. "He knocked me over." Why hadn't the man simply killed her? Maybe Alex had been too close and the thug didn't want witnesses. "He got scared when he heard you yelling."

Alex reached out his hand to help her to her feet. "I saw one of them run off in the other direction. This is a little more serious if they are going to start hurting people. Last time this happened, it was some teenagers going from farm to farm, running through the property."

So there was more than one of them. "Do you think you'll call the police?" Not that that would help her. There was a part of her that really hoped it was just teenagers, but she couldn't take chances. If there was the smallest chance she'd been found, the U.S. Marshals would need to move her.

His hand cupped underneath her elbow. "I might have to if we can't get to the bottom of this." He leaned a little closer to her. "Are you sure you're not hurt?"

She winced and touched her bruised back

muscles. "Guess I hit the ground pretty hard." Alex's concern for her warmed her heart.

"Why don't you come back to the guesthouse? I'll fix you a cup of tea and get you an ice pack. You probably don't have much in the way of supplies for the cottage yet."

"I will, but could you give me a minute? Bluebell sounds really stirred up in there. I'll make sure everything is locked up tight." She didn't want Alex to see how badly she was shaking.

He rested a hand on her shoulder. "Morgan, this really frightened you."

The warmth of his touch permeated her thin cotton shirt. She nodded but didn't say anything, afraid she wouldn't be able to keep the emotion out of her voice. Let him think it was just teenagers. She knew better.

"I'll lock up while you calm down Bluebell." His voice filled with compassion. "We'll go back to the house together."

They entered the stable. Bluebell stepped side to side in her stall. Morgan slipped into the stall, stroking her hands over the horse's neck and back. She leaned close so her side rested against the horse's front flank. She looked into Bluebell's coal dark eyes.

We're both afraid, aren't we?

"It'll be all right." Bluebell let out a heavy

snort. Her stomping subsided. Morgan leaned in close and buried her face in the horse's mane. Her eyes warmed with tears.

She had no idea how they'd found her. She had complied with the witness protection rules of not talking about her past or contacting anyone she knew in her former life. It seemed odd, though, that the assailant hadn't killed her outright. One thing was certain. She couldn't stay here.

She'd have to pack her things and call the marshals as soon as she could get a cell phone signal.

"You ready to go?" Alex closed and latched the stable door. He pulled out his ring of keys to lock the door on the other end from the outside. They lived far enough away from the city that crime wasn't a huge issue. All the same, he should have remembered to lock the doors.

"Yes, I'm ready."

Morgan didn't turn to him. Her hand went up to her face. When she did turn around, it looked to him as if she'd been crying. Clearly, she didn't want him to notice, so he didn't mention it.

In the few days she'd been working there, he'd concluded that Morgan Smith was not easy to get to know. She was friendly and connecting with clients but very closed down when it came to talking about herself.

Morgan gave the horse one final pat on the neck before climbing out of the stall. Alex had to hand it to her—she was good with the horses. He wasn't in the habit of hiring someone without references, but the day she'd arrived for the interview, she'd talked an uppity horse into taking the weight of a saddle and calmed the frightened kid who'd been dealing with that same horse.

She gazed at him, her dark brown eyes holding a world of mystery. She rubbed her lower back and winced. "That ice pack sounds really nice right now." She wore her long dark hair in a ponytail. Her cheeks flushed with color—maybe from the cold, maybe from the scare she'd just had.

They walked through the stable and out into the darkness. Only two windows in the guesthouse glowed with golden light. It was a weekday, so they only had one guest. On the weekends, all six rooms were usually full. Clients who lived in the city drove up and stayed for two or three days of riding. They were two hours outside of Des Moines in Iowa farmland. The Stables boarded horses and owned some to provide lessons. Alex's favorite part of his job was the therapeutic riding program for disabled and underprivileged children.

Morgan and Alex walked side by side onto the expansive porch of the guesthouse. He led her through an open sitting room furnished with leather couches and rough pine end tables into a large kitchen. Only he and Morgan lived on the property. He had private quarters in the guesthouse and she had the caretaker's cottage. Mrs. Stovall, who supervised the cooking for guests and cleaning of the rooms, drove in from Kirkwood, a tiny town five miles up the road. She hung up her apron promptly at seven every night.

Morgan glanced around the kitchen while he put a kettle on. "This is really homey."

He detected emotion in her voice, longing perhaps. After grabbing an ice pack from the freezer, he turned to face her. "Oh, does it remind you of a kitchen you grew up in?"

Her face blanched and she looked off to the side. "No, I just think it looks very…welcoming." Her tone was defensive.

Even that tiny bit of probing about her past scared her. She exuded confidence around the horses, but in many ways she was like a frightened little bird. What was she hiding? Everything else about her seemed honest and forthright. But still, there was a guarded quality to their interaction, as if she'd built walls around herself.

He set two mugs on the counter and pulled out the tea bags. "Mrs. Stovall's rules remain even when she's not here. We have access to everything in the kitchen, but we have to clean up after ourselves, same as the guests."

She picked up the tea bag and placed it in her cup and then pressed the ice pack against the small of her back. "Understood. I get the impression she runs a pretty tight ship."

They then talked a little more about the horses. The kettle whistled. Alex poured the steaming liquid over her tea bag and pushed the sugar dish in her direction across the counter. He watched her stir in the sugar, the metal of the spoon tinkling against the inside of the mug. Once again, he was struck by her beauty, the wide brown eyes and thick eyelashes, her swanlike neck.

But it was that look of vulnerability in those eyes that had won him over. There was no guile in her. That's why her secretiveness confused him. Was she running from an abusive boyfriend or husband?

She gazed at him over the top of the mug.

She was a horse that needed to be wooed. If she trusted him, maybe she'd open up to him. What could he talk about that wouldn't make her retreat? "Tomorrow the kids from Reach Out will be here for their therapeutic riding session."

Her eyes grew wide as though a realization had come to her. "Oh, yes, tomorrow. I saw that on the schedule."

"You should be able to handle it. We'll have five children here with varied ability levels. Each one has an aide or family member to help. I'll come out and introduce you to everyone."

"I'm looking forward to it. I like working with children."

"So you've done something like this before?" He'd blurted the question without thinking.

Her reaction was more subtle this time, though he could tell the question upset her. Her round eyes narrowed, and she placed her cup back on the counter. "Let's just say that I've always loved children and wanted to protect them." She angled away from him. "It's late, Alex. I should be getting back to the cottage." She placed the ice pack on the counter, too. She turned on her heels. He listened to the echo of her footsteps across the wooden floor of the lounge.

Feeling frustrated, Alex poured out Morgan's half-full cup of tea and washed the mugs. Maybe it wasn't an abusive boyfriend. She might be hiding from the law. He didn't want to believe that Morgan was involved in anything shady. But he didn't want to be a chump, either…not again.

He'd had enough lies in his life. His ex-wife had cheated on him for a year with his best friend before filing for divorce. Though he'd voiced suspicions, he'd believed Gretchen when she had said there was nothing going on. The deception had left a hole in his heart that would never mend.

He needed someone to deal with the day-to-day care of the horses so he could focus on the financial and promotional end of running The Stables. Plus, the Waverly Horse sale was in two days. He'd need her help picking out and hauling a horse.

Clearly, Morgan could do this job. As qualified as she was, though, he had zero tolerance for someone who couldn't be forthright with him.

TWO

Morgan glanced over at the redheaded boy staring at the ground and then at his mother, a woman of about forty.

"His name is Richie. This is his first time riding. I'm Adele." The mom gave away her nervousness with the wringing of her hands.

In the morning when she felt safe leaving the cottage to get a cell phone signal, Morgan had left a message with Brendan O'Toole, her contact at the marshals' regional office in Des Moines. Even with all the doors and windows locked she'd had a restless night's sleep. Though her nerves were on edge from the incident last night, she didn't want to leave Alex high and dry. She'd swallowed her fear, gotten dressed and gone out to do her job. The marshals would get this cleared up soon enough and move her. She felt pretty sure nothing was going to happen to her in the daylight with all these people around.

The other four children in the therapeutic riding class were already being led around the riding arena on their horses.

Hoping to ease Adele's fears, Morgan turned to face the boy. "Richie, you're going to have a great time."

Richie angled his body away from her.

"He has autism. He can't talk, but he understands every word you say to him." Adele patted the horse's neck. "I used to ride all the time when I was a girl. I hope he loves it as much as I did."

"I'm glad to hear you have some experience." Morgan studied Richie, who continued to look at the ground. "How about if we get used to the horse?"

Adele took Richie's hand and pulled him toward the horse that Morgan had already saddled. "Richie, this is Miss Smith, and she's going to help you learn to ride."

Richie nodded but didn't make eye contact. He tugged on his shirt collar.

"Richie, meet George. He's very gentle." Using slow movements, Morgan took Richie's hand and laid it flat on George's neck. She moved his hand up and down. George angled his head toward Richie and sniggered. "He likes you."

Richie grinned. Adele stepped in closer and stroked George's nose.

In her peripheral vision, Morgan noticed a dark SUV pulling up in the lot. Two people, a man and woman, got out of the car. Morgan tensed. What were Serena Summers and Josh McCall from the St. Louis Marshal's office doing here? They couldn't have gotten the message from the Des Moines office and made the long drive that fast. But, now that they were here, she could talk to them about being moved.

"Miss Smith, what's the next step?" Adele's voice pulled Morgan from her anxious thoughts.

"I'm sorry. Do you feel comfortable leading Richie around? I'll help get him into the saddle, and then I need to speak with these two people for a minute."

As Josh and Serena drew near, Morgan instructed Richie to place his foot in the stirrup. The two marshals stood off at a distance, waiting for her to finish.

After Adele led Richie toward the group, Morgan crawled over the metal fence that surrounded the outdoor arena. Why hadn't they told her they were coming? How could she ever expect to have anything that felt like a normal life if they could show up at any time?

If Alex saw them, she'd have to make up a lie about who they were.

Both Josh and Serena nodded as she approached them.

The marshals were dressed more casually than the tailored suits and crisp white shirts they'd been wearing the first time she'd met them. Serena had pulled her dark hair up with a clip and she wore jeans and a button-down shirt. Josh dressed in a windbreaker, khakis and a polo shirt.

Morgan had met them once before when she'd been told that they were the ones handling the illegal adoption ring case. Her initial impression of Josh and Serena was that they were both good at their jobs, but there was a tension between them that she didn't understand.

Morgan glanced around. It would be nice to hide in the barn while she talked to the marshals, but she couldn't leave the class in case there was a crisis. Alex was in his office in the guesthouse. Hopefully, he'd stay inside so he wouldn't wonder who Josh and Serena were. She didn't like the idea of deceiving him.

Josh spoke first. "The reason we're here is we just wrapped up a case that had some similar elements to it as yours. I don't know if you saw the news story about a woman named Emma Bullock. She was found beaten nearly to death in a Minneapolis park. She had no memory of the assault or of who she was. She went by the name of Julie Thomas for a long time."

So that's why they'd come here. They probably hadn't gotten her message yet. "I haven't had time to watch the news." She drew her attention to the students to make sure everything was running smoothly. "I don't see how that relates to what happened to me in Mexico."

Serena rested an arm on the fence. "As it turns out, Emma was trying to protect a baby at the time of the assault. Unfortunately, the baby was taken from her."

Morgan's chest tightened. More than anything, she hated that anyone would harm an innocent child. "Did they find the baby who was taken?"

Serena shook her head. The forcefulness of her words gave away how upset she was about the crime. "The missing baby's name is Kay. Does that ring any bells for you?"

Morgan closed her eyes, trying to shut out the pain connected with knowing a child had been kidnapped. She shook her head. "Is this Emma woman Kay's mother?"

"No," Serena said. "Kay's mom is a young girl named Lonnie. We've been unable to track her down either, and we're afraid she may have met with foul play.

"For a while, we thought we might have found Kay. A blonde, blue-eyed baby was brought to the Denver airport by a man we know to be associated with this ring, and it was on the same day Emma was attacked."

Josh pulled a photograph out of his jacket pocket. "As it turns out, there are two different babies. We call the little girl we intercepted in Denver Baby C. She's in foster care right now."

Morgan stared at the photo. A happy baby with a tuft of blond hair and bright eyes looked back at her.

"Does she look familiar to you?" Josh stepped toward her.

"Give her a moment to think, Josh." Serena's words were terse.

The tension between the two marshals had bubbled over. She wondered what the history was between them. It seemed personal. Maybe they had been involved at some point and weren't anymore.

Josh shot Serena a look that had daggers in it and then turned to face Morgan. "A blonde, blue-eyed baby would be unusual in Mexico."

The trauma of what she had been through made her memory foggy. "I definitely never placed a child who looked like that. But sometimes we had moms who would visit once and then change their minds."

"It would have been shortly before you had to leave Mexico," Josh said.

Morgan strained to put together a cohesive memory from that time. A vague picture materialized in her mind. "There was a mom with a blonde baby. I think the mom's first name was Vanessa."

Serena stepped closer to her, urgency filling her voice. "Do you remember her last name?"

Morgan shook her head. "If I had the records, notes and photographs from my office, I might be able to help you more." Frustration rose to the surface. "Were you able to get anything from the agency office?"

"By the time we cleared the paperwork with the Mexican authorities, the place where you said your office was had a real-estate firm occupying it. We haven't been able to locate the other woman you said worked there. Whatever you left behind got destroyed."

Could her coworker have been a part of the deception? Anger burned inside her. The agency had represented itself as Christian.

Had they used her to give the agency legitimacy? "So all you have to work with is what I witnessed."

Josh cleared his throat. "We need to connect the dots in order to get the big fish behind all of this. We're looking at multiple incidents in different states and now internationally. We put you under our protection because we believe your testimony might be valuable once our case is made."

Serena picked up where Josh left off. "It would be helpful if you could remember any more details."

The marshals weren't hiding her out of the goodness of their hearts. She was in witness protection because they thought she might be of value. "I know that you expect me to help."

Josh paced. "In all the dealings with these mothers and children, there must have been names mentioned. There has to be some sort of connection back in the States."

Morgan shook her head. "We dealt with a lot of different agencies and people." She tried to piece the memories together... "That night Josef attacked me in the office, I was going through the records. There was a pattern with three of the women, meeting with me and then deciding to keep their babies. And then a few weeks later, they'd be back ready to give up their kid. When they came back, they seemed agitated and afraid."

Josh crossed his arms over his chest. "So you think they might have been blackmailed or coerced?"

Morgan nodded. "I noticed other things, too. My coworker started transporting the babies across the border to meet the adoptive parents. Adoptive parents are supposed to meet residency requirements in Mexico—they can't just have their babies delivered."

Josh shoved his hands in his pockets. Both of them must be mulling over what she had told them. "When you showed up, I thought maybe you'd gotten a message from my local contact," Morgan said.

Josh looked at her. "Brendan never called us."

"Last night at least two guys were prowling around the grounds. They tapped on my window and tried to open my door. Then when I was outside, one of them knocked me over." Her voice tinged with anxiety. "Do you think whoever this big boss is could have found me already and sent someone?"

Josh seemed alarmed. "What happened after he knocked you over?"

"He ran off because Alex was coming

around the corner. Alex thinks it was just teenagers goofing around, but I don't know."

Josh's voice grew intense. "Did you get a look at him?"

"All I saw was his plaid coat," Morgan said.

"That's not much to go on." Serena faced Morgan. "We can look into it from the angle of information having leaked out. I don't think any details about your relocation have been shared with anyone outside the St. Louis office except with Brendan. If there's even the possibility you've been found, we'll move you."

Josh looked directly at Morgan. "*You* haven't said anything to anyone, have you?"

Morgan grew nervous, remembering how Alex had pressed her for details about her past. "No, I haven't let anything slip."

Serena glanced at the children in the class and the surrounding buildings. "Do you like it here, Morgan?"

"I do. I love it." She'd hate having to leave. "It reminds me of where I grew up. It's just that there are children here, and I wouldn't want them being hurt at my expense." Or Alex.

"Morgan, we'll do everything to ensure you're safe here." Serena's gaze was unwavering. "For today, we'll stay in the area until we can clear this up."

"We can check with local authorities. Find out if any other properties had prowlers. If it was teenagers, they might have decided to make a night of it," said Josh as they headed out of the stall. "Call Brendan if you're worried.

Serena and Josh headed back toward their car.

She listened to their footsteps fade as she turned her attention back to the class.

"Looks like the therapy riding class is going fine." Alex had come up behind her without her noticing.

Again she looked at the student riders being led around the arena. "Yes, they seem to be doing pretty good. I haven't had to jump in at all."

"It's pretty self-regulating once you get it started." He studied her for a moment. "Who were those people you were talking to?"

Morgan turned away from Alex, gripping the top of the fence for support. "They were friends from Des Moines." She squeezed her eyes shut, hating herself for lying.

"Maybe they could come out riding sometime."

"Yes, that would be nice." Her stomach coiled into tight knots.

"Listen, I've got a kid who's going to come and help you with some of the manual labor a few days after school and on weekends. He's worked for me for almost a year. Craig has some issues but he's a hard worker, and I feel he deserves a chance. His father has had his share of heartbreak, most of them due to a drinking problem."

In that moment she saw Alex's heart. He wanted to give a troubled kid something better than what he had. "Everyone deserves a chance." She turned her attention back to the class.

"I'm not throwing too much at you at once, am I? You seem distracted," Alex said.

Richie had a big grin on his face as he rode George around the arena. The sun warmed her skin. She did like it here. It would be a shame to have to leave. She looked into Alex's brown eyes. "No, Alex, you're doing fine. I'm sorry if I'm not focusing like I should."

Morgan looked out at the parking lot where Josh and Serena had just pulled out. Another slow-moving car went by on the road. At first, she thought the car was going to pull into the lot. Instead, it eased past.

The hair on the back of her neck electrified and she felt a chill that had nothing to do with the temperature of the air. Why was the driver going so slowly? What was he looking for?

Alex touched her upper arm. “Something wrong?”

She shook her head, remembering Serena’s reassurance. “It’s nothing.”

“Good then. Craig should be here later this afternoon.”

“I’m looking forward to meeting him,” Morgan said.

“Tomorrow I’m going to the Waverly horse sale. I have funds to purchase another therapy horse. I’d value your opinion on picking one out.”

A horse sale meant crowds. And Waverly was one of the biggest in the Midwest. Even she had heard of it. “Isn’t there work to do around here?”

“No classes scheduled. We’ll get the horses squared away in the morning and head out.”

“Okay.” Her response sounded halfhearted. She might not even be here tomorrow.

“After you’re done with the class, there are some horses that need to be exercised. We try to make sure the boarded horses get out at least every other day. There’s a roster posted in the stable that shows when each horse was last exercised.”

Fear danced at the corners of her mind. She

didn't like the idea of riding alone when the marshals still hadn't cleared up who the late-night prowlers were. "I suppose I can do that."

Alex stepped toward her, concern etched on his face. "Are you sure everything is all right?"

She'd have to get beyond her own fear if she was going to do this job even if it was just for another day. "No, I'm fine." And she'd have to learn to stuff her emotions a little better. Alex was way too tuned in to what she was feeling even when she tried to hide it.

Alex turned to go. She watched him amble back to the guesthouse.

Feeling uneasy, she returned to the class to help the students finish up and take the horses back to the stable to remove the saddles. She worked in the stable with no sign of Craig or word from the marshals. Alex had hired her to do a job.

Despite her fears, Morgan saddled up one of the boarded horses that needed to be exercised and headed for the trails that surrounded the property. The irony wasn't lost on her that the horse she chose to ride was named Anxious Heart.

She could see a trail that looked like it led in a wide arc around the property with very little brush to obscure her view of the stable and outbuildings. She'd be able to see someone coming toward her from a long way off. She'd have time to get back to relative safety of the stable and other people.

She started Anxious off at a light canter. Sensing that the horse wanted to go faster, she pushed him into a gallop that turned into a hard run. The harder she pushed the horse, the faster he went.

She glanced side to side. She was the only one out here. Gradually, her anxiety subsided.

Out here in the quiet with only the steady rhythm of the horse's hooves, she could forget herself. She could convince herself that the faster she rode, the further her trouble would be away from her. She could outrun the loss and the fear.

Anxious showed signs of tiring. Morgan let up on the reins and sat up straighter in the saddle. A light rain sprinkled from the sky when she turned onto the trail that led back to the stables. A calm washed over her that made her think she could make it through the rest of the day while she waited to see if the marshals would relocate her.

When she led Anxious Heart through the open door of the stable, she spotted a teenage boy hammering a nail into a loose board on a stall gate.

"You must be Craig."

"Yup." The boy didn't stop working. He was a tall, thin kid with hair that was blond on top and black on the bottom. He looked to be about fourteen.

Morgan walked toward him. "Alex probably told you. I'm Morgan."

Craig stalked across the floor and picked up a bucket. When he finally looked at her, she saw hostility in his eyes.

The response took her aback. Alex had said that Craig had some issues. She decided not to do anything to feed his bad mood, whatever it was about. "Well, it looks like you know what you're doing. Alex said you've worked here awhile."

Craig let go of the bucket, causing it to clatter when it hit the dirt floor. "I've been doing this job for eight months now."

His anger toward her was off-putting, but she refused to play into it. Her response was soft. "That's wonderful. You'll probably be able to teach me a few things."

Craig drew his mouth into a tight line and wrinkled his nose. He leaned over, picked up the bucket and stomped off toward the other end of the stable.

Morgan led Anxious Heart into his stall, pulled his saddle off and started his rubdown.

In light of everything she was dealing with, she could handle one ornery teenager. A few minutes later, Craig left the stable without explanation. Morgan finished getting Anxious Heart settled in and walked toward the entrance of the stable, taking the time to stroke the noses of the horses who wanted the attention.

A coat that must belong to Craig hung on a hook by the door. Morgan examined the plaid pattern. The same one she seen last night when she'd been knocked over. Through the open door, she saw Craig filling the troughs in the corral with water. The coat was probably a common enough one, but it would have to be a pretty big coincidence if it wasn't him who'd tried to scare her last night. The discovery eased her fear, but she'd have to find out for sure before she called Josh and Serena.

Alex walked across the grounds toward her. "So you've met Craig."

"Yes, I met him." Morgan shaded her eyes from the sun. "I think it was Craig who was prowling around last night."

Alex nodded. "What makes you say that?"

"His coat is the same one the guy who knocked me over was wearing. Craig and his friend wanted to scare me last night."

Alex shook his head as his expression hardened. "I'm surprised he did that, but I think I know why. Craig mentioned that his dad would like the caretaker's job. Robert Jones has plenty of experience with horses, but he's not reliable," Alex said.

"I guess that explains why he was so hostile toward me just now. He views me as the person who stole his dad's job."

Alex seemed incensed. "He has no right to treat you badly."

She appreciated his defense of her. It was kind of chivalrous, actually. She grabbed his hand at the wrist. "You said yourself he's a good worker. Maybe he needed to blow off some steam, and that will be the end of it."

Admiration shone in Alex's eyes. "It's your call."

"'A soft answer turns away much wrath.'" The verse had come easily enough to her mind, an old habit.

His face brightened. "Proverbs 15:1. I know it well."

He looked at her at though he was waiting for her to say something more. A spark of connection had passed between them. But even that was a lie. She'd lost everything in Mexico, including her faith. She had wanted to make a difference in the world and instead she had unwittingly aided in children being taken from their mothers. "It's a really common verse. I don't know why I even said it."

He took a step back. Her harsh response may have stunned him. "I've got some bags of feed to unload."

It was better that she not foster even a small connection to him. The marshals had warned her against forming any attachments. "Do you need my help?"

"I'll get Craig to give me a hand," Alex said. "Maybe I'll have a word with him about what he did last night and tell him he needs to drop the attitude going forward."

"How about I do it?" she said. "Maybe I can build a bridge." Given Craig's background and what Alex had said about him, she was willing to give him a second chance.

"Suit yourself. But if he gives you any more trouble, let me know. I can unload the feed myself." He ambled across the yard.

She stood watching Alex take bags of feed off the back of the truck. Alex was what her dad would have called "a good hand," a man who wasn't afraid of physical work.

She walked toward the shed where she had seen Craig go. Alex thought they had something in common when she'd uttered the Bible verse. He had no idea how all of that now rang hollow for her. She longed to get back to the place where faith was as comfortable as a pair of broken-in boots, but she didn't know if she ever would. Disillusionment had taken up residence in her life.

She stood at the opening of the shed. Craig had his back to her, but she could tell he was holding something. He turned slightly and she saw a kitten cupped in his hands. When Craig looked up and saw Morgan, all the warmth and softness evaporated from his expression.

"What are you looking at?" Craig sneered.

"Are you taking care of those kittens?" She stepped toward him. He had made a bed for a mother and her three babies.

"Alex lets me keep them here. My dad says cats are freeloaders." His words were harsh and defensive, and he even seemed a little embarrassed.

She reached over and petted the kitten Craig held. "Do you kind of wish your dad would have gotten my job?" She understood Craig's motivation. His father having a job would probably eliminate some of the shame associated with having a parent who drank too much. The job would have made his father look respectable...or maybe it was more simple, a financial need.

Craig's features compressed, revealing

harsh lines. He pulled the kitten away from her. "What do you care?"

"Was it you who tried to scare me last night?"

"So what if it was," he snapped. "It should be me and my dad living in that house."

Morgan stared down at the black-and-white cat licking one of her calico babies. For a brief moment, she'd seen a different side to Craig. He was capable of compassion. He deserved a chance. "How about we wipe the slate clean and start over? Last night never happened."

Craig offered a halfhearted shrug. "Whatever."

His posture and words were defensive, but she thought she saw just a flash of gratitude in his eyes. It was a start.

She stepped out of the shed and headed back to the barn. She took in a breath of straw-scented air and began to feel a little more relaxed about staying at The Stables. Alex had been right about the late-night prowlers. The knowledge that she hadn't been found made her feel more confident about the Waverly horse sale and going out in public. Maybe a day spent helping Alex would be fun.

THREE

A chill hung in the air as Alex made his way to the stable. Morgan was already busy filling feed buckets when he stepped inside.

She looked up at him. "Hey, thought I'd get an early start. You wanted to be out of here by eight, right?"

She wore a denim coat with a lacy white top underneath and jeans. He grabbed a bucket off the wall and filled it with feed from a bin. "Thought I'd come out here and give you a hand, but you've got most of it done."

He stroked the neck of one of the horses and then stepped inside the stall to look at a cut on its back leg. He helped Morgan finish with the feeding and watering. They worked quickly and quietly. When they stepped outside their breath came out in puffs in the cold morning air.

Morgan crossed her hands over her body. "Hope it warms up. This is cold for April."

"It's Iowa," Alex said.

"Where I grew up in Wyoming it was cold, too, but this chill cuts through to my bones."

It was the first piece of personal information she'd shared with him. He counted it a victory that she had even opened up to him that much. Maybe she was starting to trust him. "Wyoming, huh?"

A worried look came across her face. "All I meant was that it's cold out here." Her voice was monotone.

Her defenses went up so quickly. "I've already got the trailer hitched up." He pointed toward the truck just beyond one of the corrals.

They drove through light highway traffic with Alex doing most of the talking. He shared his plans for repair and expansion of The Stables and his desire to grow the therapeutic riding part of the business.

Morgan offered words of encouragement and stared out the window at the passing landscape.

It was nice to talk to someone who understood his passion for how the horses could change lives.

Parking was at a premium despite their early arrival. This was the third day of a sale that would last a whole week. Though the bidding took place in the indoor arenas, they walked past a dirt lot where horses pulling buggies and riders on horses circled around.

Alex explained. "Gets the horses exercised, works out their nerves so they show better, plus potential buyers have a chance to see the horses in action."

They made their way through the throng of people. Morgan seemed to grow more nervous. He saw fear in her eyes.

He touched her arm lightly. "Not much of a crowd person, huh?"

She nodded, edging closer to him. A cluster of people at the entrance jostled and pushed. He placed a protective hand on her back.

He leaned close and spoke into her ear. He could smell the light floral scent of her perfume. "It'll seem less crowded once we get inside."

The sale was set up with dozens of bidding arenas where the horses were paraded past the potential buyers. "The auction for the horses that might meet our needs won't happen for a while." He held up a catalog that contained a listing of all the horses for sale. "We can go down to the corral where they're kept and have a look at them before the sale."

They pushed through the crowd past a sign that indicated draft horses were being auctioned off. Morgan peered inside the arena. "Draft horses are so beautiful."

"We have time to watch them. Why don't we go have a seat?"

Morgan seemed to relax when they sat down. After a description of the draft horses, some single, some in pairs, and indication of the bloodlines, the auctioneer started the bidding while each horse was led back and forth in front of the spectators. A pair of draft horses went by with a rider standing on top of them, one leg on each horse's back.

Morgan laughed and grabbed his arm. "Didn't know I was going to see a circus act, too."

It was good to see her enjoy herself. They shared some popcorn Alex had bought from a vendor who was walking through the bleachers. His shoulder pressed against hers. He glanced sideways at her. She blushed and turned slightly.

The glow of attraction didn't surprise him. He'd thought she was beautiful from the moment he'd hired her. He liked that she had let her guard down even a little bit. The attraction wasn't anything he would act on, though. After what his ex-wife had put him through, his desire for a romantic relationship was close to zero. Still, he felt at ease around her.

Maybe Morgan was running or hiding from someone. But he'd come to The Stables to escape, too. After Gretchen left him, the prospect of sitting behind a desk all day only added to his depression. He'd chosen to do that sort of dependable job for her anyway. The owners of The Stables hired him for his finance and marketing skills, but it was being around the horses that appealed to him most. Chalk it up to some boyhood dream of being a cowboy. He'd found an unexpected measure of happiness at The Stables. Maybe Morgan could, too.

Morgan glanced around at the crowd. Her mood seemed to shift slightly as she stared straight ahead.

"Everything all right?"

"Yes, fine." She bit her lower lip. "I think I'll go use the little girl's room."

Alex pointed off to the side of the arena. "Careful, you have to walk past the horses waiting to enter the arena."

As he watched her descend the bleachers, he wondered what had stolen her good mood so quickly.

Morgan glanced up at the bleachers as she pushed through the crowd that had gathered on the floor of the arena. Up in the stands,

Alex turned slightly to speak to the man next to him. She'd been having a pleasant time with him when she'd felt the press of a gaze on her. When she turned around, a man had stepped down the bleacher stairs and tapped the woman in front of her on the shoulder.

A false alarm. She was in a constant state of vigilance. Even her slip with Alex in telling him she was from Wyoming made her cringe. The information was benign enough, but she could not get into the habit of telling anyone who she used to be. The truth was, she felt relaxed around Alex. She wanted to share with him.

Morgan squeezed around several clusters of people.

"Wait a second, lady." A burly man in a checked shirt with the sleeves cut off stuck his arm out to block her.

Becoming more aware of her surroundings, she stuttered in her step. She heard the screeching of metal and stomping of hooves. Two draft horses were led past her and into the arena. People crowded in on both sides of the entrance for the horses. The horse already in the arena must have been taken out the other side. Her heart beat a little faster at the sight of the huge animals.

The burly man pulled his arm toward his

body. "Just didn't want you to get stomped to bits."

She nodded and walked past the gate, now closed, where a large grey Percheron stomped the dirt and nuzzled its handler.

Morgan used the restroom and then stepped outside. She was headed back toward the bleachers when she saw a man in a beige baseball hat standing by the restrooms. His eyes bore through her. He was a big man, built like a heavyweight boxer. The look of murder in his eyes reminded her of the look she'd seen in Josef Flores's eyes in Mexico.

A group of women came between her and the man. When the women disappeared into the bathroom, the man in the baseball hat was gone. She took several steps back toward the bleachers. The gates screeched open and another draft horse thundered by. The animal yanked suddenly away from the handler and the crowd dispersed like cockroaches in the light. Panicked cries rose up. Morgan's heart beat a little faster.

The handler regained control and three other men swarmed in to help. Once the spirited horse was secured in the arena, Morgan made her way to the bleachers. She spotted the beige hat moving through the crowd in front of her. On instinct, she pivoted. She couldn't go back to the bleachers. If this man was after her, she'd be putting Alex in danger.

She scanned the area looking for a security guard. What would she tell them anyway, that a man in a baseball hat was staring at her in a menacing way?

To calm her nerves, she walked outside past several corrals containing different breeds of horses from quarter horses to miniatures and ponies. She crossed her arms over her chest and kept up a brisk pace until peace overtook the rising panic.

It's not like beige was a unique color. Plenty of people probably wore that kind of hat. Still, the memory of the man's sinister eyes narrowing as he looked at her made her keep walking. She stopped at a corral filled with Clydesdales. She watched owners and trainers bridle horses and lead them around the corral.

The day had warmed and the sun soothed her nerves. She closed her eyes. She had to let go of the notion that someone could come after her. The marshals knew what they were doing. Her fears about the prowlers had proved to be unfounded. Still, the memory of Josef's words to her echoed in her brain: *I will find you and kill you.*

She opened her eyes and watched the

horses awhile longer. A cluster of people slowly dispersed, leaving only a few stragglers. The man in the cap stood across the corral. Her breath caught even as her heart rate soared. He'd pulled his cap down so all she saw of his face was shadow and chin.

The man stepped in her direction.

She turned to run, smashing against hard muscle.

Alex gazed down at her. "What's going on?"

"I...um...ah..." When she glanced across the corral, the man in the hat had vanished.

"You're shaking." He gripped her hands, his voice filled with concern.

Morgan struggled to pull it together, to at least manage the veneer of calm. What explanation could she possibly offer? "I thought somebody was following me, but I was wrong."

He squeezed her hands a little tighter. "When I saw you turn the other way, I thought maybe you'd gone to check out the horses."

She looked into his warm gentle eyes. She couldn't lie to this man again, so she said nothing.

His voice held only compassion. "I can see that this has you upset. Why don't we find a place to get a cup of coffee, and then we'll go have a look at those horses?"

He demanded no answers or explanation from her for why she was so afraid. "I'm all right. Let's go see the horses." Being around the horses would help her regroup faster than a cup of coffee.

"Okay, we can do that." He let go of her hands and scanned the corrals. "I think the lot that we want to look at is right over there."

They walked through the labyrinth of corrals and spectators until they arrived at a fenced-in area containing six horses. "These horses are older quarter horses," Alex explained. "Not showy, but good temperament."

"You want a horse that doesn't spook easily and is responsive to an inexperienced rider." Morgan gripped the top railing of the fence as she studied the horses. "You can't really tell much about them by standing here. Can I go in the corral?"

Alex shrugged. "I have no idea what the rules are about that. I guess you can do it at your own peril."

As soon as she stepped into the corral, a sense of peace returned. She wandered among the horses, gauging their response to her, looking into their eyes, stroking their necks and backs, watching their reaction when she stepped into their peripheral vision. Horses tended to get jumpy when they thought something was coming at them from the side.

She patted the neck and mane of a chestnut gelding. "This one, I think."

Alex flipped through his catalog. "That guy's name is Chipper's Boy."

She stroked Chipper's nose as he leaned into her touch. She looked into his dark eyes. "You'd love those kids, wouldn't you?"

"Let's go get settled so we can bid on him." Alex's voice fell softly on her ears. She glanced over at him and saw admiration in his eyes.

For the rest of the sale, Morgan kept looking over her shoulder trying to hide her anxiety from Alex. Why couldn't she let go of her suspicions?

Three hours later, they were headed home with Chipper's Boy loaded in the trailer.

Morgan settled into the passenger seat of the truck. She studied the curve of Alex's ear, the laugh lines around his mouth and eyes. The way his cowboy hat angled slightly to the left. Alex focused on the road ahead.

She appreciated that he hadn't pressed her for answers she couldn't give. He had a gentle unassuming quality that made him easy to be around.

"I had a good day," said Morgan.

"Me, too," he said. "The horses are my favorite part of the job."

"But you don't get to spend as much time with the horses as you'd like?"

"Take the good with the bad. It beats sitting in an office with no windows ten hours a day."

"Is that what you used to do?"

"I worked for a financial firm. I like an office without walls or windows."

She laughed. "I like wide-open spaces best, too. I feel like I can get a deep breath." Something they had in common. "What was the reason for the job change?"

His jaw tightened. "That was a lifetime ago."

She detected a twinge of pain in his words. Even he had things he didn't want to talk about. So they both had secrets.

Alex checked his side and rearview mirrors. Morgan craned her neck.

"That car's been behind us for a while." She purged her voice of the fear that settled in her stomach.

Alex nodded. "Seems like it, doesn't it? Probably just a man headed in the same direction as us."

And maybe she had just imagined that the

man in the baseball hat was following her. Her heightened awareness made her assume things, which only fueled her fears. She had to let go, had to learn to relax.

You're safe now, Morgan. You're safe.

She wanted to believe that.

FOUR

Alex's hand curled into a fist and tension knotted up his back as he stared across the corral. He didn't have to hear the conversation between Morgan and Craig to know that Craig was giving her trouble. The teen's body language and snarling expression revealed the tone of the exchange.

Morgan had asked Alex not to interfere. She wanted to win Craig over on her terms. He wanted to respect her wishes, but it took every ounce of restraint he had not to jump in. Twin twelve-year-old girls waited for their first riding lesson. Morgan had saddled the first horse and pointed toward Craig to get the second saddle off the fence. The boy rested his arm on the fence and lifted his chin in defiance of her request.

That was it. He didn't like seeing Morgan treated this way. This kid was out of line. Alex jumped over the post fence and stalked toward the saddle. He lifted it with a sideways glance toward Craig. "There's a stall gate latch that needs to be repaired. Why don't you go take care of that?"

"Sure, Mr. Reardon. I can do that for *you*." After a disdainful glance toward Morgan, Craig meandered through the corral toward the gate.

Alex flung the saddle over the second horse while the two girls, Debbie and Doris, waited off to one side.

"Thanks, Alex," said Morgan. The exasperation was evident in her voice as she looked over at Craig entering the stable. She turned her attention back toward her students. "Since you watched me do the first saddle, why don't both of you come over and do the second one?"

The girls grimaced at each other, shrugged their shoulders and trudged toward the horse.

"Don't be afraid," Alex encouraged.

Both of the girls had ginger hair and an abundance of freckles. They stepped toward the horse, consulting each other in whispered tones. Doris had been the more talkative of the twins when their mother had dropped them off. Now both of them had fallen silent as they glanced nervously at Morgan.

"Doris, grab the front strap from underneath the horse and cinch it up," Alex said.

His prompting seemed to trigger their memory for what they were supposed to do.

Morgan stood beside Alex but spoke to the twins. "Go ahead and run through the steps. I'll stop you if I see anything incorrect." Morgan crossed her arms and continued to watch the girls while she leaned in to talk to Alex. "Craig would have gotten the saddle for me eventually. He's just testing his boundaries."

"I couldn't stand to watch it. And I don't like the way he's treating you."

Morgan raised her voice. "Debbie, remember you don't want any of that strap hanging loose. Hook the stirrup to the saddle horn if that makes it easier to see." She watched for a moment. "There you go."

Debbie turned toward Morgan and grinned at her mistake, jerking her shoulders up to her ears while her cheeks turned red.

Alex continued to speak in a hushed tone while he kept his eyes on the twins. "I could find a dozen other kids in town who want this job and wouldn't be this kind of trouble."

"You said yourself you want to help him. His conflict is with me." Morgan grabbed Alex's wrist. "Please, don't fire him. I think the money from this job is the only income he and his father have right now. Craig mentioned something this morning about his father losing his janitorial job."

Alex felt a pang of guilt. He wanted the kid to have a shot at something better than what he had, but Morgan didn't deserve to be disrespected. "I'm not going to stand by and watch him mess with you like that. He needs to know that's not right."

Doris raised her hands in triumph. "We got it." She turned to her sister for a high five.

"Give him some time," Morgan said in a low voice before walking over to the girls. "Let's check the tightness on the front and back strap." Morgan placed her fingers between the saddle strap and the horse. "Good job—tight enough so it's not going to fall off, but loose enough so it won't dig into the horse's side."

"I can't wait to race," said Debbie.

Morgan laughed. "I appreciate the enthusiasm, but you gotta walk before you run, honey. Alex and I will lead you ladies around the arena and then you can ride on your own in there. Maybe for your second lesson, we'll hit the trails." Morgan glanced over at Alex. "Does that work for you?"

Morgan's dark eyes danced with delight. She had a natural teaching ability. He had a pile of paperwork to deal with, but he would much rather be out here in the warm sun helping someone discover how wonderful riding could be. Being out here with Morgan made it doubly nice. Whatever task was at hand, they worked well together. “Morgan is right. We don’t want to rush anything.”

“Good then,” said Morgan. “Doris, go stand by your horse and Alex will show you how to get on.”

While they led the twins around the outdoor arena, Craig came out of the stable and then disappeared around the side. He returned a few minutes later holding a gas can.

Wonder what he’s up to.

He needed to let go of his suspicions. If Morgan was willing to be patient with the boy, he could be, too.

Morgan’s laughter pulled him from his thoughts. She handed the reins up to Debbie. “I think you’re ready for a little solo. Remember not to hold the reins too tight.”

Alex saw fear flash across Doris’s face. “Just a gentle walk around the arena. We’ll be right here watching,” he reassured.

“Remember what I said. The horses are very sensitive to your signals.” Morgan stepped backward without turning away from the twins.

Doris nodded and pressed her heels into the horse's belly. Debbie took off a moment later. They bounced in the saddle, not matching their movements to the rhythm of the horse.

Morgan leaned back against the fence close to where Alex stood. Her proximity reminded him of that initial flush of attraction he'd felt at the horse sale.

"We should be seeing it any minute," Alex said as he watched the girls circle the arena.

"See what?" She leaned even closer to him.

"The smile." He tilted his head toward Debbie. "Wait for it." Debbie's features compressed into a look of extreme concentration. She circled the arena several more times. With each round, her stiff posture relaxed as did the tightness of her expression. By her third time around the arena, a smile formed on her face. He'd seen it a thousand times.

"Favorite part of my job," he said.

"You have a teacher's heart." Morgan pressed her back against the fence and propped a leg up on a lower rung.

The look of contentment he saw on her face made him smile. He wanted to know her better. "Did you have any brothers and sisters when you were growing up in Wyoming?"

She pushed herself off the fence, the delight melting from her countenance. "Alex, you have to stop. I'm happy to answer any question that relates to this job, but don't pry into my personal life."

Her voice was like the cold edge of a knife slicing through him. The question had risen from natural curiosity. That's how friendships grew, by getting to know more about a person. "I didn't mean to step out of bounds."

Her words were softer than before. "Maybe we should just focus on the work that we have to do here." Her eyes held a pleading quality, as though she wanted to say more.

A dozen theories floated through his head about why she was such a fortress. He could entertain all sorts of speculations about who Morgan Smith was. None of it helped him to get to know her better. She wasn't interested in sharing about herself. The bottom line was she didn't want anything but a professional relationship with him. "I wasn't intending to be nosy." He held out his hand to her. "Truce."

She shook his hand. Her fingers feathered lightly over his calloused palm. "Truce."

Heat rose up his neck in response to her touch. "Back to work for both of us."

She pulled free of his grip. "I need to get these girls off the horses in time for their mom's return. I've got four horses yet that need to be exercised."

"Four?" Exercising four horses would be a full day for one person. Craig's duties didn't extend to riding the horses.

"Yes, Bluebell hasn't been ridden for a couple of days. I've taken her out as often as I can. I have yet to meet Bluebell's owner. Does he or she ever come out to ride that beautiful animal?"

"Bluebell belongs to a woman named Stephanie. She's boarded the horse for six months. I think I've seen her half a dozen times." He turned back toward the guesthouse.

"She's not a bad horse, just high-strung. She needs someone to work with her." Morgan sounded indignant. "That really is the owner's responsibility."

He agreed that Stephanie wasn't a very responsible owner, but he had to keep his opinions about his clients to himself. Today was Friday. The guests would be showing up soon, and the weekend would be nonstop interaction and work with lots of people wanting to ride. Morgan was already shouldering a lot of the work duties. "Tell you what. I'll go inside and get a few things done. By the time you've gotten the twins' horses settled and finished the lesson, I can come back out and we'll take the horses out together."

"Having company always makes the time go faster." A faint smile graced her full mouth. "I'll have the horses saddled up and ready." He watched her walk back toward the twins, her long dark hair waving in the wind.

Was he a glutton for punishment or what? She'd just made it abundantly clear that she didn't want him butting into her life, yet he'd looked for an excuse to spend time with her.

He shook his head and strode back toward the guesthouse.

After helping the twins unsaddle, rub down their horses and clamber into the car with their mother, Morgan returned to the stable. She hadn't seen Craig since he'd left the lesson and stomped off to the stable. Despite his attitude, the boy did have a strong work ethic. He was probably in one of the other buildings doing whatever repairs needed to be done. Morgan picked up two bridles off the hay bale where she had instructed the twins to leave them.

Most of the tack was stored in narrow locked cabinets on the opposite wall from the horse stalls. Morgan retrieved a key and opened the door to the cabinet. A scraping sound caused her to take a step back. A spur that had been hooked to the cupboard door fell into the hay by her feet.

She picked up the spur and fingered the star-shaped rowel, which was designed to dig into a horse to make him go faster. Use of spurs was not a method she favored. If she hadn't moved in time, the metal could have cut her or damaged an eye. No one would accidently put a spur up there.

Would Craig be so malicious as to do something like that, knowing that she was the only one who had a key to the tack cupboard? She debated whether to tell Alex or not. He was already on the verge of firing the kid. And what if she was wrong? What if a careless client had placed the spur up there? She would have no chance of winning Craig over. As resentful as the boy was, she just couldn't picture him doing anything that would harm her physically. His defiance was much more up front.

Maybe it would be best not to tell Alex. She shook her head when she thought about him.

A spark of attraction had passed between them when he'd held her hand to call a truce. The fluttering of her heart at his touch caught her by surprise. The last thing she needed to do was fall for the boss. She touched her hand to her heart as the familiar sadness returned.

If she couldn't talk about who she used to be, how could she get close to anyone? Connection happened when two people fully knew each other. That wasn't going to happen…not until all of this was over and the people behind the baby-smuggling ring were caught.

At least Alex seemed to finally understand that she didn't want to talk about the past. The marshals had suggested that she create a new background in addition to having a new name. She couldn't bring herself to live with that much falsehood. When she had first moved to Des Moines, she thought the best strategy would be to keep her distance from everyone. But then an intense loneliness had set in.

Here at The Stables, working with the children and the horses alleviated the loneliness and loss of purpose. Alex was the only one who had asked any probing questions.

Bluebell whinnied from her stall. "You're raring to go, aren't you?" She retrieved the horse's bridle and slipped it over Bluebell's head. The horse stretched her neck over the stall gate, and Morgan stroked her nose and neck.

Bluebell jerked her head back violently and shifted her weight from side to side. The metal of her bridle clinked with each head thrust. Several other horses stirred in their stalls. A thumping noise came from the loft. Morgan lifted her head. She smelled smoke. She sprinted toward the door, searching for the source of the fire.

Bluebell reared and kicked the gate of her stall. Frantic, Morgan opened the door. There was no fire outside. The smell of the smoke was much more intense inside. Her gaze traveled upward toward the loft, where smoke billowed out. Grabbing a wool saddle blanket, she climbed up the ladder. The fire was small but spreading quickly, fueled by the hay spread across the floor.

She placed the blanket over the flames, smothering them. She coughed as the smoke grew thicker. Pressing her forearm over her mouth, she whirled around. The flames had jumped to a straw bale. She could feel herself growing lightheaded as she picked up the wool blanket and stumbled toward the spreading flames.

Down below, wood splintered as Bluebell crashed through her stall. Heavy smoke surrounded Morgan. She coughed, struggling to beat back the flames. She felt dizzy as she swayed and slumped to the floor of the loft.

FIVE

When he emerged from the guesthouse, Alex scanned the fence by the stable expecting to see two saddled horses. What could have delayed Morgan? His walk turned into a run when he saw smoke coming out of the loft window. He ran to the far side of the stable where the large sliding door was.

He tilted his head. “Morgan?”

Silence.

He pushed open the door. The pounding of hooves assaulted him right before the black Arabian charged toward him. He stumbled out of the way. He could catch Bluebell later. He darted into the barn. Though agitated, all the other horses were still in their stalls. No sign of Morgan. He lifted his head and saw that smoke floated out from the loft.

He climbed up the ladder. His heart stopped as fear shot through him at lightning speed. Morgan lay on her side not moving.

He rushed over to her. Flames that had consumed a straw bale raged across the floorboards. Coughing from the thickening smoke, he gathered Morgan into his arms, flung her over his shoulder and carried her down the ladder.

Craig waited for him at the bottom with a hose. "I saw the smoke coming out of the loft window. I called the fire department."

"Good." Alex focused on Morgan as Craig climbed the ladder with the hose.

He carried Morgan outside and laid her in the grass. When he touched the side of her neck, he felt a faint pulse. He patted her cheek. "Morgan." She stirred and coughed. Dark eyes locked onto him as relief spread through him. "Hey."

She still wasn't coherent, and he couldn't tell the extent of the injuries, but she was conscious.

Craig called down from the loft window. "I could use some help up here."

Morgan closed her eyes. He didn't want to leave her until he was sure she would be all right.

Craig called down a second time. "It's getting a little out of control."

"I have to help him. Can you sit up?" She

nodded and he reached out, pulling her up and supporting her back.

"I'm all right." Her voice was hoarse. "Go help Craig."

He glanced around, looking for a way to assist Craig in putting out the fire. "I'll be back to check on you."

He grabbed a bucket and filled it from an outdoor trough.

By the time the fire department arrived, they had put out most of the flames. The bulk of the damage was to the straw bales that had been stored in the loft. The treated wood of the barn had not burned as quickly as the straw. The whole place smelled like smoke, though.

With the firemen dealing with the last little bit of the fire, he climbed down to the main floor of the barn. Craig waited for him at the bottom. Sweat stained the boy's shirt, and his face glistened. He had a smear of charcoal across his forehead.

Alex cupped Craig's shoulder. "Thanks for your quick thinking."

Craig nodded.

"What happened, anyway?"

The boy shrugged. "I was cutting the grass up by the guesthouse when I saw the smoke."

He recalled seeing Craig with the gas can as suspicion niggled at the edge of his mind.

How deep did the kid's anger run? Then again, Craig had shown up right away to help.

"What were you doing with that gas can earlier?"

Craig tilted his head as though he were assessing what the intent of the question was. "I was getting gas for the lawn mower." His answer was defensive.

His explanation made sense. If not Craig, then who? Lessons had finished a while ago. Mrs. Stovall and her crew were busy in the guesthouse getting ready for the weekend guests. One of them could have slipped out, but why would they want to set the loft on fire? "I need to go check on Morgan."

Craig sneered. "You might want to ask *her* how this fire got started."

"I doubt Morgan had anything to do with this." Everyone was playing the blame game. The firemen would have a clearer idea of what caused the fire. "It's still kind of smoky in here. Let's get these horses out into the fresh air."

He helped Craig get the remaining horses out of their stalls and led them to a nearby corral.

When he glanced up the road, several guests had parked in the lot and were staring in the direction of the fire trucks, shielding their eyes from the sun. Alex groaned inwardly. The last thing he needed was for the guests to think this place was unsafe. He'd deal with that fallout in a minute. First he needed to check on Morgan.

He found her sitting on a bench with a fireman's blanket around her. Gripping a water bottle, she stared at the ground. His heart surged with joy to see that she had recovered so quickly. She looked up. Her eyes brightened when she saw him.

"Hey, how are you doing?"

She touched her neck. "The fireman said there's probably some damage from inhaling the smoke."

He sat down beside her. "I'm glad to see you made it."

"Was there any doubt?"

"You weren't conscious when I found you in the loft." Talking about what had happened made his throat tighten with emotion. He'd had a flash image of his life without Morgan, and it had scared him. "I had a moment there." Affection fused with his words.

"I'm glad you came when you did." She gazed at him, her expression warm and welcoming, but then when she looked toward the stable that worried look distorted her features. “What happened? Why would a fire start up there?”

“I’m not sure. The firemen should be able to figure out the cause.”

She coughed and took a sip of water. “I hope they do.” She sounded almost fearful.

“Me, too.” He didn’t want to make accusations unless he could be sure. “Did you notice anything when you were in there?”

She looked away. “Not with the fire, but I think we need to have a talk with Craig. Someone put a spur on top of the tack cupboard. I nearly got my face sliced open.”

Alex clenched his jaw. “This is getting serious. If he’s doing stuff like that, he has to go.”

“I agree. It’s one thing to be surly with me. It’s another to try to hurt me.”

Another car pulled into the lot. Alex raised his head. He knew that car. “I think we have a bigger problem than figuring out how the fire got started.”

Morgan followed the line of his gaze. “What do you mean?”

Alex stood up. “Bluebell broke out of her stall when the fire started.” He pointed at a blonde woman strutting toward the stable. “And that is Bluebell’s owner, Stephanie Bliss.”

* * *

Morgan rose to her feet to stand beside Alex. A second woman got out of the passenger side of Stephanie's luxury car. After glancing at the fire truck, Stephanie waved at Alex and made a beeline for him.

"Here we go," said Alex, tension evident in his voice. "She's a difficult client anyway. She won't like the news about her horse."

As the women drew closer, Morgan saw that they were dressed in jeans that looked like they'd just been pulled off the rack, crisp button shirts and bulky, expensive-looking necklaces. The other woman was a brunette, but she sported the same hairstyle as Stephanie and held her designer handbag in the crook of her elbow just like Stephanie.

"Alex, it's so good to see you. This is my friend Melody. She flew in from L.A., and she loves to ride. I can't wait to show her Bluebell. Can we rent one of your horses so she can ride, too?"

Alex shifted his weight. "I'm sorry, you weren't on the guest list for the weekend. We don't have any more space.'"

"This was totally spur-of-the-moment. Besides, we'll be staying at a hotel in town." Stephanie wrinkled her nose. "We want to get in a massage and a nice dinner after a day of riding."

Stephanie lifted her chin and looked down at Morgan. "So is this the woman who is going to get Bluebell saddled up for me?"

Alex cleared his throat. "We had a little bit of excitement this afternoon. There was a small fire in the stable loft."

"Oh, yes, I see that." Stephanie narrowed her eyes at Morgan.

Morgan jumped in. "Bluebell got spooked, broke down her stall and took off."

Stephanie's mouth formed a perfect *O*. She crossed her arms. "What are you saying?"

"We'll get the horse back, no problem." Alex remained calm. "They usually don't run far."

Stephanie adjusted the sunglasses on her head. "I'm ready to ride right now, Alex."

Morgan could feel her ire growing. So far, Stephanie had expressed no concern for the horse. She hadn't even asked if Bluebell was okay.

"I'm so sorry for the delay. We should be able to catch her sometime today and you'll have all day Saturday and Sunday to ride." Despite Stephanie's rising irritation, Alex kept his tone polite.

Stephanie let out a huff of air. "Sometime

today? Don't you mean you're going out right now to find her?"

"I understand your concern. We'll get to it as quickly as we can," Alex said.

Irritation simmered inside Morgan. She didn't like the way Stephanie spoke to Alex.

Stephanie waved her hands in the air. "I don't know what kind of place this is that you let the horses get away like that."

That was it. Did this woman have no understanding of what they had just been through? Did she even care about Bluebell? "I think the important thing is that your horse is all right. A little spooked is all."

Stephanie put her hands on her hips and glared at Morgan. "Excuse me, I came here to ride my horse."

Every muscle in Morgan's body tensed. She was going to snap if she had to talk to this woman one second longer. Stephanie was one of those people who treated people and animals as if they were there to do her bidding. "It has been weeks since you were here. Horses need attention. They're not inanimate objects."

Stephanie's well-groomed eyebrows shot up. "So now you're blaming your incompetence on me. I don't pay these ridiculous prices to be told this is my fault."

"I wasn't suggesting that. The horse shouldn't have gotten away. I'm only saying that you have to work with a horse like Bluebell, build a connection, make an effort." Her voice had slipped into a higher register.

Stephanie inhaled and exhaled so intensely that her nostrils ballooned. "Alex, why are you letting this woman talk to me like that?"

Alex's calm demeanor never wavered. "We'll get the horse for you." He wrapped his fingers around Morgan's upper arm. "Morgan and I are going to take care of it right now."

Stephanie rolled her eyes. "Fine. I guess Melody and I can go into town and shop for a while."

Morgan planted her feet. Bluebell deserved better than Stephanie, but Stephanie was what she had to work with. She spoke more gently to Stephanie. "Please, think about what I said." What Morgan cared about was the horse.

Obviously ruffled, Stephanie pursed her lips and then opened her mouth to speak.

"Let's go round that horse up." Alex grabbed Morgan by the elbow and led her away before Stephanie could respond.

Morgan clenched her teeth. Why hadn't Alex backed her up? She glanced over her shoulder as Stephanie and her friend strutted back to the parking lot. "Was I wrong?"

"No, you're right. If you own a horse like Bluebell, you have to be willing to invest time in her," Alex said.

"So why didn't you say that to Stephanie?" Her voice faltered. Alex not taking her side hurt more than she wanted to admit.

"You don't stay in business by constantly speaking your mind, Morgan." He leaned closer to her. "She had a right to be upset. We weren't taking care of her horse like we should have. Haven't you heard the adage the customer is always right?"

She stepped away, pulling free of his grip on her elbow. The intensity of her emotions was unsettling. If she didn't care for Alex, her reaction wouldn't have been this strong. "Let's go find that horse."

"Fine, I'll get the truck. You saddle up one of the other horses that needed to be exercised. We'll kill two birds with one stone. I'll get Craig to help the guests who want to go out right away."

Morgan entered the stable to get the tack. The firemen no longer occupied the loft. Outside, she heard their truck backing up. The stable still smelled faintly like smoke. Morgan walked over to the corral where the horses were and placed a bridle on Anxious Heart and then saddled him up. She led the horse out of the corral as Alex stood beside his truck talking to one of the firemen.

Alex wrapped up his conversation and patted the fireman on the back. He turned toward Morgan. "You ready to go?"

She nodded and pulled Anxious a little closer to the truck. "What did he say about the cause of the fire?" Fear surrounded her question. From the moment she'd seen the fire, she wondered if someone had started it to kill her. She was the one who was in the stable all the time. Maybe they'd put the spur in such a dangerous place to disable her, too.

Alex shook his head. "He couldn't say for sure. He found the remnant of some paint rags. If there had been a spark from something, that might have started it."

"Who put the paint rags up there?"

"Who knows? There's always a construction job going on around here. Stuff gets tossed up there when people don't know what to do with it." His voice held a note of exasperation.

She had to find out how the fire got started. "What kind of spark would he be talking about, anyway?"

Alex shrugged. "Something electrical would

have done it." He yanked open the door of his truck. "The fireman said it didn't look like gasoline was used as an accelerant. If it had been, the place might have burned to the ground. It was probably just an accident."

It was natural for him to assume the fire was accidental, but she wasn't so sure. "Are they going to do any kind of investigation?"

"Morgan, it was a small fire. They have better things to do with their time. We've got to catch this horse. I didn't need this kind of delay. Guests are coming in." He climbed into the cab and slammed the door.

She could tell he was getting impatient. She spoke through the rolled-down window of the truck cab. "Good then, I'll take the trails and I assume you'll cover the dirt road."

He started his truck and then shouted over the sputtering roar of the engine. "Call when you find her."

Morgan got up on Anxious Heart and directed him toward the trails. Alex had been so abrupt. She understood that he was feeling tension over things going wrong. What bothered her was that his mood affected her. Despite her best efforts, he was becoming more than just a boss. She liked spending time with him and she cared about what he thought of her. She cared about *him*.

Morgan pushed the horse into a gallop as she surveyed the landscape. In the distance, she could see the dust cloud that Alex's truck stirred up. She had no idea how many acres connected with The Stables. The trails she'd gone on continued for miles. How hard would it be to find one high-strung black horse?

Not wanting to tire out Anxious, she slowed to a trot. Alex didn't seem too concerned about the fire, but she couldn't let it go. What if someone had started the fire on purpose? She considered Craig, but she really didn't think he would do something like that. That wasn't his game. He liked The Stables and he liked the horses. It was Morgan he had a beef with. The thumping noise she'd heard when she'd entered the stables could have been another person jumping out of the loft window. At the very least, she'd have to call Brendan and tell him about it.

As her horse's hooves pounded out a rhythm on the hard-packed trail, fear stirred inside her. She wasn't crazy about being out here on the trail alone.

SIX

"I found her." The soft airy tones of Morgan's voice caressed Alex's ear through the phone. "She's in some brush by the north fence. I can see a gray farm house off to the west."

At least Bluebell hadn't wandered onto someone else's farm. "Great. I'm about a five-minute drive from there."

"Don't worry about it, Alex." Her voice reverberated across the line. "I can bring her in since you have so much work to do."

Alex let out a heavy breath. He caught the tinge of pain in her voice. He hadn't meant for his frustration with everything going wrong to be taken out on her. The liability for losing a boarded horse was huge, and Stephanie didn't strike him as the kind of woman who would extend him any level of mercy.

"I can handle it," she said when he didn't answer.

He did have a lot to do, and she was perfectly capable of bringing in a horse on her own. "All right then. I'll see you back at the stable in a little bit. I'm sure a lot of people are going to need help getting saddled up."

She offered him a quick goodbye and hung up.

Alex's old truck rumbled down the road. He did an abrupt U-turn and headed back to where Morgan was. Regardless of how much work he had to do, he owed her an apology. He parked the truck far enough away to prevent spooking Bluebell and hiked toward the area Morgan had described.

From a distance, he saw Morgan slowly step toward Bluebell. She held her palm open, probably with some sort of treat. The other hand held a rope, which she rested on her thigh. Bluebell reared up and then stepped side to side but didn't bolt.

Morgan stopped about ten feet from Bluebell and waited for the horse to come to her. She slipped the rope over the horse's head while it ate from her hand.

He loved watching her work with the horses almost as much he liked being with the horses himself. So much of his life felt like a giant detour. This is what he had been meant to do. Gretchen had never liked the outdoors or animals, but he'd grown up spending every chance he got on his uncle's farm. He stepped a little closer to them.

Morgan leaned toward the horse and said, "I have half a mind to run away with you myself. Then we'd both be safe."

A twig snapped under his boot, and both Morgan and Bluebell startled.

Morgan raised her head. "I didn't see you there."

She'd been really focused in on the horse. "Sorry, I didn't want to destroy your horse-whisperer moment."

Morgan stroked the horse's neck and then stopped, abruptly stepping around to the side of Bluebell. "What happened here? Looks like she got cut up by some brush or something."

Alex cringed. The cuts were right where a saddle needed to go. "Stephanie's not going to be happy." He was mad at himself for letting things get so out of hand.

"She can't be ridden until she heals. I don't care how it makes Stephanie feel." Her voice was forceful.

"Agreed, but let me handle giving her the news that she came all the way down here for nothing," Alex said.

Morgan brushed Bluebell's forelock with her hand. "Sometimes people need to hear things straight or they don't hear them at all."

It had taken guts to tell Stephanie she needed to care more about her horse. He admired that. "You'd never make it in business. It's all about the word choice." He chuckled and walked the few paces to where Morgan had tethered Anxious Heart.

"Diplomacy was never my forte. I can't help it. I have to speak my mind if I think something is wrong." She took the reins of the horse from him. "Why'd you come back here, anyway?"

"To say I was sorry."

"I understand about business and all that." She looked directly at him. "Guess I wanted to feel like you were on my side." Her eyes held a warm quality that drew him in, and he wondered if she wasn't trying to tell him more than she was saying.

He cupped his hand on her shoulder. "I'm always on your side, Morgan."

"Thank you. I needed that." Her eyes glazed. Something had her upset. What was she keeping from him?

He focused on the soft curves of her lips. Whatever was causing her so much pain, he wished she would share it with him. He leaned closer, wanting to hold her.

Bluebell whinnied and tossed her head.

The moment shattered and Morgan stepped

back. "You'd better get back to running things. I can bring her in on my own."

He strode back to his truck with a glance over his shoulder. Morgan focused on getting on Anxious Heart and leading Bluebell.

He jumped into the cab and slammed the door. What had he been thinking? He wanted to hold her, but he couldn't fall for someone who wouldn't even give him details about her family.

He looked in the rearview mirror as Morgan and the two horses got smaller. He had to let go of the blossoming feelings he had for her. There were too many unanswered questions where Morgan Smith was concerned. He didn't want to be set up for any kind of deception.

As the stable and outbuildings came into sight, he wondered what she'd meant when she said if she ran away, she'd be safe.

By the time Morgan returned and led the horses toward the stable, she could hear the sound of music coming from outside the guesthouse. Some sort of barbecue was taking place. Two men played guitars and sang while twenty or so people milled around picnic tables.

Inside the stable, the gate Bluebell had

busted down had already been repaired. She had to hand it to Craig—the kid wasn't afraid of work. She led Bluebell into the stall and put some salve on the cut.

Hopefully, Alex had given Stephanie the bad news with more tact than she would have been able to muster up. She pulled the saddle off Anxious Heart and led him into his stall. Her muscles ached and her throat still hurt from inhaling smoke. She looked forward to a quiet dinner and then maybe she could get one more horse exercised before dark.

Alex greeted her when she stepped outside. "You want to join us for dinner? Mrs. Stovall has whipped up her famous barbecued pork and corn on the cob."

"Is it part of my job description?"

"It's an opportunity for the regular guests to get to know you," Alex said.

"I was hoping to catch a quick dinner alone so I could take one more horse out. I'm not crazy about exercising a horse in the dark alone." In the past, a late-night ride would have been relaxing. Now it only made her feel vulnerable. Maybe the fire was only an accident, but she needed to talk to the marshals.

"I still owe you help with exercising the horses," Alex said. "Even if it's dark, I'll go out with you. Now, why don't you come enjoy the meal?"

Alex had already put in a long day, too. His offer to help made her forget their earlier squabble. "Okay. I never turn down barbecue."

Alex's face brightened. "Let's go eat."

They walked toward the party. "So did you give Stephanie the bad news?"

"Her feathers were a little ruffled, but she took it better than I thought she would," said Alex. "I think she was starting to think shopping and fancy meals would be a lot more fun for her and her friend anyway."

The tangy aroma of barbecue sauce made Morgan's mouth water. Alex took her hand and led her to a plus-size woman with white fluffy hair pulled into a bun. "Morgan, this is Mrs. Stovall."

Mrs. Stovall grabbed Morgan's hand and squeezed it tight. "Pleased to meet you." She had a smile that was mostly teeth and dancing brown eyes. Her grip nearly shut off the circulation in Morgan's hand. "You look like you could use some meat on your bones."

After Mrs. Stovall loaded up Morgan's plate, Alex introduced her to several of the guests. She didn't see Craig anywhere. Talking to him about the spur would have to wait.

Morgan enjoyed the good food and visiting. The guitar player switched to slower tunes as the guests filtered away and the sky turned gray. Some people returned to the parking lot and left while others disappeared into the guesthouse. About ten or so people lingered, conversing in hushed tones as it grew dark.

Alex rested a hand on her shoulder. "I think we can slip away now."

"Great. I'll go get the horses saddled," Morgan said.

"I'll meet you there in about ten minutes."

Inside the stable, Morgan found a middle-aged man brushing a horse. He was short, and his cowboy hat was pushed back on his head revealing a widow's peak.

"Hi, I'm Morgan Smith, the new horse caretaker. You must be Sunny's owner." She pointed to the silver dapple horse.

The man nodded. "I got off work a little late. I was hoping to take her out, but now it's getting dark. I'll go out first thing in the morning."

"Alex and I are exercising some horses. You're welcome to join us on the trail."

"Naw, I'm a little worn out." He stroked his horse's neck. "I have the weekend to ride. I'm Leonard, by the way."

Morgan nodded. "Glad to meet you."

"I try to get up here every weekend. I love spending time with Sunny. I'd keep her in my condo in the city if I could, but, you know, all those silly large-pet regulations."

Morgan laughed. Leonard was the kind of horse owner she liked, someone who respected that the animals needed time and attention.

The sky had turned dark by the time she led Jojo and Chipper's Boy outside. She tethered the horses to the fence and looked around for Alex. White Christmas lights twinkled around the patio where the barbecue had taken place. A few people sat in lounge chairs.

She saw movement in her peripheral vision as her attention was drawn toward the caretaker's cottage. A man, shrouded in shadow, peeked into her living room window.

She ran toward the cottage. "Hey."

The man looked up and then disappeared around the side of the house. Her heart pounding, she took a step back and moved toward the safety of the people who were still outside.

Alex met her half way. "Everything all right?"

She struggled to keep her voice calm. "Someone was looking in my window."

"Happens all the time. The guests are curious. They don't see the Private Residence sign."

"You think so?" Doubt plagued her. Why would the man run off like that? The explanations came easily enough for Alex. To anyone else, they would make sense. As soon as she was done helping Alex, she needed to talk to the marshals about the fire and now this man.

As she stuck her foot in the stirrup and swung her leg over Jojo, she realized how alone she was in all this. The marshals would protect her physical safety, but she had no one she could talk to about her fear. She couldn't call her father or siblings or anyone she'd known as a missionary to talk through her fear and concerns. All this would be so much easier and maybe she'd be less jumpy if she didn't have to face it by herself.

A sadness settled into her bones. How much longer would it be like this? Always looking over her shoulder, never relaxing.

Alex came up beside her on his horse. "Here, slap this on your wrists. It's reflective tape so we can see each other. I already put some on the horses' saddles and legs."

Moving single file, they headed out on the trail. As the horses trotted at a steady pace, Morgan felt the tension leave her muscles. She gazed up at the sparkling night sky, and then at Alex. Having him close soothed her raw nerves. They passed one other rider headed back toward the house. Morgan recognized him as one of the men who had been at the barbecue.

Even when the trail widened and they were able to ride side by side, they didn't talk. Alex seemed to understand that a night ride like this was an opportunity to regroup. Pointless chatter would only destroy the serenity of the moment. Gradually, her fear subsided. She took in a deep breath, appreciating the cool, clean fresh air.

"Let's give these guys a good workout." Alex spurred his horse into a trot and Morgan followed suit.

Morgan enjoyed the challenge of keeping up with Alex, who was an excellent rider. As they edged toward a clump of trees and a river, Alex reigned in Chipper's Boy. He shifted his weight in the saddle and tilted his head. "I love nights like this. It's a good chance to pray out here in the vast silence, don't you think?"

Morgan closed her eyes. She could at least not lead him on about where her faith was at. "I don't pray much anymore."

He sat up straighter in his saddle. "Oh, why is that?"

"Let's just say that things have happened in my life that make it hard for me to pray." Her words came out with unexpected intensity as the events in Mexico played out in her head.

"Been there, done that. They don't make a T-shirt for it," Alex said.

Morgan laughed in spite of the seriousness of the discussion. His reaction surprised her. "Guess I'm in good company then." Alex seemed so grounded in his faith, yet even he had been plagued by doubts at one point. She wondered what had happened to test his faith.

"You can get through it, Morgan. God's not afraid of your honesty. You can shout at him if you need to, just don't stop talking to him."

His words were like a healing balm to her. His not pressing her for the details behind her disillusionment only made her want to talk to him more. The longing to tell him the whole story was so intense, her chest felt like it was in a vise.

I wish I could share everything with you, Alex.

A few drops of rain sprinkled from the sky. Within minutes, the rain intensified.

"Boy, that storm came out of nowhere. We'd better head on back." Alex pulled up on the reins and turned his horse around. They pushed the horses into a gallop. The trail quickly became slick and muddy. Rain soaked through her thin jacket. Alex increased his speed, but Jojo didn't have the same stamina as Chipper's Boy.

Lightning flashed in the sky. Thunder crackled. Jojo reared up. Morgan held on. The reflective tape on Alex's horse was all she could make out in front of her. The rain became a downpour as Morgan egged Jojo on. The horse grew edgier and then bolted suddenly from the trail. Morgan's attempts at steering the horse back only stirred her up more.

More lightning and thunder caused the horse to take off at a hard run. Morgan held on and leaned forward until Jojo ran out of steam. The horse continued to show signs of agitation, stepping sideways and jerking her head. The thunder and lightning had really spooked the horse. Morgan slipped out of the saddle and soothed the horse until she calmed down.

"Now let's try to get home before there's any more lightning." The rain soaked through to her shirt as a chill blanketed her skin. She looked around. They'd veered off the trail and nothing looked familiar to her in the dark.

Morgan got back on the horse and headed in the direction they had come, scanning the dark landscape for a landmark that might orient her.

She heard the sound of an approaching horse. Alex must have come back for her.

"Alex, over here." Could he even hear her above the rain?

The rider did not respond but the clopping hooves grew louder. As the silhouette of a horse and rider came into view, the hairs on the back of Morgan's neck prickled. A sense of dread filled her.

It wasn't Alex.

SEVEN

Alex craned his neck, expecting to see the glow of reflective tape behind him. He pulled up on the reins and waited for a moment, thinking she would come into view. He turned his horse around and headed back up the trail. He shouted Morgan's name but the words seemed to fall at his feet. Sound wouldn't carry far in the harsh wind.

How could he lose sight of her so quickly? The last time he'd looked over his shoulder she was right behind him. He continued back up the trail, his anxiety growing. He was really starting to care for her but her secrecy concerned him. They'd shared a moment of connection back at the river. She'd opened the door just a crack. And he'd been reluctant to share the details of his own dark night of the soul when Gretchen had left him, so Morgan wasn't the only one who was clammed up about the past.

He reined in his horse and jumped off where the trail appeared marred. He examined the ground. Hard to tell with the conditions changing quickly from the heavy downpour. The horseshoe patterns suggested that her horse might have been spooked and headed off the main trail.

He studied the ground, looking for more clues as to which direction she could have gone. This part of the land was heavy with brush. The horse would take the path of least resistance. He jumped back on Chipper's Boy and steered through the open areas.

As his horse wove around the brush, he knew that shouting her name would be futile. He peered out from beneath his cowboy hat as the rain pattered on top of it. He saw a flash in the distance, probably the reflective tape. Alex spurred his horse to go a little faster.

The rain had soaked through his clothes. In no time, they'd be back at home drying off in front of a fire. He spurred his horse to go faster. His optimism faded when he didn't see the reflective tape again.

He hurried toward where he'd seen the first flash, hoping nothing had gone wrong.

Morgan sat up straighter in the saddle. The rider had not heard her cries and had disappeared into the brush. Maybe Leonard had decided to bring Sunny out for a ride after all and had been caught in the rain, too. She was alone and shivering from the cold and wet. Alex must be looking for her, though. She hadn't been on these tangent trails and none of the landmarks looked familiar in the dark.

Jojo skittered to one side. The storm still had her upset. She kicked Jojo into a trot and headed in the general direction of the main trail. The light from the stables should come into view sooner or later.

After ten minutes of riding, panic set in. She didn't see any light or even any landmark that could guide her home. The trail was slick with mud. She couldn't risk injuring the horse. She slowed to a trot. She thought about the fire and the man she'd seen earlier around her house. Those memories and the darkness only fed her fear.

Jojo stopped abruptly at the creek bed, pitching Morgan over the top of her into the river. Morgan stood up only to be knocked down by a torrent of water. A hand grabbed her arm and pulled her toward the shore. Fear sank in like the teeth of a lion.

"Leave me alone!" She hit the rider's chest hard.

The rider released her. "Hey, hey." The voice was Alex's. "I didn't want you to drown."

Shivering, Morgan wiped the water from her face. She hadn't realized that thinking about the man by her house had made her so afraid. "Jojo bolted…and I got lost." Her voice trembled.

Alex gripped her arms above the elbow. His voice filled with compassion. "It could have happened to anyone."

The strength of Alex's touch and sound of his voice warmed her despite the rain.

"You were really scared there."

"Yes, I didn't realize how easy it was to get disoriented." More than anything, she wished she could explain to him why she was so on edge.

"Let's ride these horses back to the barn so we can get warmed up."

Morgan reached for Jojo's reins. The horse jerked away and whinnied. "I really don't think Jojo can stand to be ridden. She's pretty spooked, and if there is any more lightning, she'll bolt again."

"I understand." Alex mounted his horse. "The storm has made her jumpy. We can lead her in." He scooted forward in the saddle and held out a hand, indicating that she should get on his horse. Leading Jojo, she placed her foot in the stirrup and swung up behind him. She wrapped her free hand around his middle.

"Settled?"

"Yes." Still shivering, she rested her cheek against his back. His wet hair brushed across her cheek when he turned his head.

He patted her hand as his horse lumbered forward. The steady rhythm of the horse's steps combined with the downpour surrounded her like a song. She closed her eyes, realizing how easy it was to be close to Alex. She felt safe with him.

Ten minutes later when she peered over his shoulder, the effervescent glow from the guesthouse came into view. They'd arrived at the stable entrance. She slid off and pushed open the stable door so the horses could go in. Her wet clothes clung to her body and added five pounds of extra weight. She was shivering so badly her teeth chattered. She was freezing, but the horses had to take priority.

They pulled saddles and bridles off the horses and placed blankets over them.

Morgan rubbed Jojo's soft nose. "Nice and cozy. Now it's my turn to get warmed up."

"I'm sure there's a good fire started in the guesthouse great room if you want to come in," Alex said.

She really didn't have the energy to visit

with the guests anymore. "I think I'll go back to the cottage and take a nice hot shower, maybe have a cup of tea."

"Suit yourself," he said. He lingered for a moment. With the darkness surrounding them, she felt the pull of attraction toward this kind man.

There was so much she longed to say to him. Heartache sunk in. If only she'd met him at another time in her life.

I do care about you, Alex.

"See you in the morning." He turned and walked toward the guesthouse.

Morgan dragged her weary body back to the cottage. She showered, letting the hot water beat on her chilled skin, then pulled on sweats. When she stepped into her bedroom, she noticed the corner of the bedspread was folded back. Something she would never do. Her heart pounded a little faster. The stack of books she kept by her bed looked askew. Had someone been in her room?

A knock sounded at her door. She moved to go answer it when something cold brushed by her bare toe. Morgan looked down as a snake slithered over her foot. Her heart seized.

"Morgan, it's me." Alex must be standing close to the door. His voice was loud.

She cleared her throat and shouted. “Alex!” Fear splintered the word into three syllables.

She heard the door burst open and pounding footsteps.

“In here.” She stood still, not even daring to breathe.

Alex appeared in the doorway. He looked down at the snake. “Don’t move.” He disappeared.

The snake trailed over her toes as Morgan released a shaky breath.

Alex returned a moment later with a hatchet in his hands. In one swift motion, he kneeled down, chopped the head off the snake and picked up its back end. She heard him stomp outside only to return a moment later to dispose of the head by sweeping it into a paper bag.

With her heart still pounding wildly, she stepped into the living room. She couldn’t stop shaking.

Alex came back through the front door, which he had left open. “I disposed of him.”

“What was it?” Her words came out as a harsh whisper. Feeling cold all over again, she hugged herself.

“A massasauga, pit viper.” He stepped a little closer to her.

“Is it… Is it poisonous?”

He nodded. Her knees felt wobbly as the black spots in front of her eyes multiplied. His arms surrounded her before she hit the floor. He helped her to the couch and touched her cheek. "That was quite a scare. Don't know how it got in here. Must be a hole somewhere. I'll have to look into that."

Morgan felt herself going numb. She stared at the floor. "Do you get a lot of those around here?"

"Out on the trail, but not in the buildings." Concern etched through his words. "They're kind of shy."

Her mind reeled. How had that snake gotten in her bedroom? She looked up at him, still trying to process what had happened. "What were you doing with a hatchet?"

"It's from your porch, to split wood. I was going to come over and build a fire for you."

She looked at the man in front of her, his broad shoulders and soft smile. If he hadn't come along… "Yes, a fire would be nice." Still in shock from what had happened, she walked toward the kitchen. "I can fix you a cup of cocoa if you like."

Alex wadded up some newspaper from a stack and tossed it in the fireplace. Her hand trembled as she turned the burner on and placed the kettle on the stove.

She needed to tell the marshals about all that had happened today. She could hear the marshals' argument in her head. They would say that if someone had been sent to get rid of her, why not just kill her outright? She agreed with that logic, but something was going on here. First the fire and now the snake.

Was it possible someone was trying to kill her and make it look like an accident?

She watched Alex stack the wood in a pyramid shape around the newspaper and light it. At least she had a small reprieve. She was safe as long as Alex was here with her. Yet another reason to be grateful for him.

She dreaded the long night ahead.

The fire was roaring by the time Morgan brought him a steaming cup of cocoa.

She settled in the chair by the fire. "That throws out some heat."

He scooted back from the flames. "Yeah, it's nice. That chill gets in your bones. Takes quite a bit to feel warmed up again." Though she tried to hide it, Alex could tell Morgan was still upset. Her gaze darted around the room while she sat with a rigid posture.

She took a sip of her cocoa as the fire crackled. "So what's on the agenda for tomorrow?" She was trying to get past her fear, but the strain in her voice was obvious.

He rose to his feet and rested his hand on the fireplace mantel. "Just more looking out for guests." Had he been too forward in offering to build the fire for her? He didn't feel comfortable leaving her alone after the scare she'd had. And she'd invited him to have cocoa. She seemed to want him to stay for a while. "We usually try to organize a couple of group trail rides. The guests forming friendships with each other keeps them coming back."

Morgan nodded. "Sounds like fun."

Alex clenched his teeth. He didn't want to talk about work. All they ever seemed to talk about was work. They'd been through a trying day together. He wanted to know her in a deeper way. If he was really honest with himself, that was why he'd wanted to build the fire in the first place.

Lightning lit up the front window and thunder crackled through the sky. Morgan jumped.

She seemed so on edge. He wished he could hold her, comfort her. "Not a fan of thunderstorms, huh?"

She ran her finger up and down her mug. "Me and Jojo both."

"Sorry about that. Maybe I should have put you on Chipper's Boy. Jojo usually isn't that wild. Course she's a young horse who's probably never been in a thunderstorm." His attempt at small talk did nothing to calm Morgan down. He remembered how she had attacked him when he'd tried to pull her out of the river. More and more, he was starting to think she'd escaped an abusive relationship. Would she even let him hold her? "I wish we could talk about something more than work."

"Like what?" Already, she sounded guarded. She swung around, accidently knocking the cup of cocoa off the table where she'd set it. "Oh dear." The sadness in her voice seemed overblown for a spilled cup of cocoa.

He hurried to the kitchen and grabbed two towels. "It's no big deal, Morgan." He tossed her one of the towels.

"But I broke the cup." She sounded as if she was about to burst into tears.

Keeping his tone light, he tried to reassure her. "They're easy to replace. Mrs. Stovall buys them by the crateful."

She swiped the towel over the spilled liquid while he picked up the broken pieces of the mug. Her movements were quick and sharp.

He had a feeling this was about more than a broken cup.

He rested a hand on her shoulder. "Seriously, it's no big deal."

She didn't pull away from his touch but continued to stare at the floor. "I'm sorry…I just…this storm and the snake."

"Yeah, it was a pretty action-packed day." After tossing the shards of the mug in the garbage can, Alex reached out for the cloth Morgan held. "Let me finish this. Why don't you sit down and catch your breath?"

"Thank you." She met his gaze, her eyes an ocean of feelings hidden behind a veil. Without thinking, he reached up and brushed his hand lightly over her cheek. She closed her eyes, seeming to welcome his touch. He shook himself free of the magnetic power of his attraction to her. You couldn't care about someone you didn't know…and Morgan had expressed zero desire to reveal any part of herself to him. He focused his attention on cleaning up the mess. She scooted away and sat back in the chair.

He rose to his feet, strode back to the kitchen and rinsed out the towel.

She got to her feet and stood on the other side of the kitchen counter. "So which one of the guests comes up every weekend?"

As he wrung out the dishtowel, he could feel his irritation growing. The guests, the horses, the work that needed to be done. Their conversations were three inches deep. He wanted more.

"You know what, Morgan? It's been a difficult day for both of us. I think I'll go get some sleep. We'll need to be up early in the morning." He twisted the remaining water out of the towel and hung it up on the stove rack.

Her voice tinged with hurt. "Yes, I guess you're right."

He stomped toward the door. "I left a few more logs for you on the porch if you want to keep that fire going for a while."

He flung open the door and stepped out into the rain-drenched night. As he made his way back to the guesthouse, he didn't care that the rain soaked through his clothes again.

Why couldn't he kill the feelings he had for hcr? Caring about her was such a dead end. Feeling a rising sense of frustration, he did an abrupt turn toward the stable. Morgan had him so stirred up, so confused. Being with the horses always calmed his nerves. He wasn't ready to paint on a smile and be with the guests who were still up.

What was Morgan's story? She sure wasn't going to tell him. He stepped into the dim stable and breathed in the hay and horse-scented air. He had a detective friend in Des Moines. Maybe his friend could find out who Morgan Smith really was.

Morgan jerked awake. From the couch where she'd been sleeping, she could see the fire was only glowing embers. She couldn't bring herself to sleep in the bedroom, not after that snake had been in there. She sat up and glanced toward the kitchen clock—5:00 a.m. Her sleep had been fitful and intermittent. Every gust of wind against the windows had made her jump and she had dreamt about babies being taken from their mother's arms. Even now when she was awake their crying echoed in her head.

She sat up on the couch and hugged herself. She'd felt safe when Alex was here. Yet she'd sent him such mixed signals, he'd been angry when he left. She didn't blame him. They couldn't talk about anything that mattered.

She had to shut down the moment between them when he'd looked into her eyes and she thought he might kiss her. She liked him. He was a decent, good man. He deserved a woman who could tell him the truth about herself. That certainly wasn't her.

Morgan rose and paced the floor. She'd called the marshals' office to tell them about the fire and the snake, but Serena and Josh were off duty. The marshal she talked to was reassuring and said he would pass on the message so they could look into it.

The hardest part about witness protection was how alone she felt. She longed to talk to her father; just to hear his voice would be a comfort.

Morgan slumped back down on the couch, trying to free herself of the restlessness that plagued her. If she could just share with one other person! Though it was an hour earlier in Wyoming, her father would already be up having his cup of coffee. He kept what he called rancher's hours. It was calving season, so his hours were even longer. Her teenage brother and sister were still at home. In an hour or so, they'd be up to help out with morning chores and catch the school bus. Seeing them in her mind's eye, thinking about them, made her heart ache.

She pictured her father stirring his cup of percolated coffee and watching the sun come up while he planned his day. The marshals had told her to cut off all ties with her past life. Her father hadn't heard from her in months even though he'd been informed that she was in hiding. She didn't like the idea of causing him pain. He'd been through enough when breast cancer had taken her mother.

She picked up the phone, pressed it against her chest and closed her eyes. It would be so easy to call him. Even hearing his voice would give her the strength to continue. She slammed the phone into the cradle.

She paced the floor and then stopped to peer into her bedroom. She stared at the cut in the wooden floor where Alex had brought the hatchet down on the snake. As isolated events, the things that had happened today could be seen as accidents.

She grabbed her raincoat. Staying here didn't feel safe anymore. She gathered a few personal items and some clothes and tossed them in her suitcase.

She dashed toward her car and pulled out on the road. She checked several times to make sure she wasn't being followed. There was no traffic at this hour. Rain came down in a soft drizzle. She whizzed past the Come and Get It Café, where the windows were completely dark and the parking lot was empty.

Was all this loneliness and all the fear worth it? She wanted to help the investigation. She wanted to know that no more babies would be torn from their mother's arms just because they were young and poor. She wanted Baby C and Baby Kay to be with their mothers. She wanted justice as badly as Josh and Serena did. Sometimes, though, it felt like such a high price to pay.

The windshield wipers drummed out a steady rhythm. As she drove, she came up with a plan. She'd find someplace to hide and then get in touch with the marshals.

Rain came down harder, and she strained to see through the windshield.

She had to be honest with herself; she wasn't leaving just because there was a chance she'd been found. It was getting harder and harder to keep things from Alex. Not because he was prying like he had been at first, but because she liked him. She wanted him to know who she was. The desire was getting harder to resist.

She focused intently on the road. Headlights filled the image in the rearview mirror. Morgan slowed down as the car crept up until it was parallel to her.

But the car didn't zoom past. It swerved toward her.

Fear building, she steered closer to the edge of the road. The other car eased into her lane, breaking off her side mirror. Her arm muscles strained as her heart pounded. The other car tapped the door of her car. The hit was enough to send her off the road and rolling downhill.

The front of her car rammed into something hard as her upper body was propelled forward and then whipped back. Everything went black around her.

EIGHT

"So what is your help doing running off at the crack of dawn?" Ralph, one of the older guests who came almost every weekend, caught Alex by the arm on his way out of the guesthouse door.

"What are you talking about?"

"I was up early walking the grounds, keeping my old-man hours like I always do, when I saw your help take off in her car from her little house. I assumed she was on some kind of early-morning food run, but she hasn't come back yet."

Alex maintained a calm veneer as his mind raced. "Thanks for that information. I'll check into it."

As soon as he could get away, he went looking for Morgan. His first thought was that she had up and left in the night. Maybe he'd been too harsh with her or maybe whatever she was being so secretive about had caught up with her and she had to leave. The possibilities tumbled through his head as he stalked across the grounds to the caretaker's cottage. He pounded on the door, not really expecting her to answer. Her car was not in the designated space by the cottage.

He tried her cell phone but got no answer.

He hurried over to his own car. He didn't like the idea of losing her for whatever reason. He had to admit—if she was gone, there would be a huge hole in his life. As secretive as she was, he'd come to value spending time with her.

He climbed into his truck and turned out onto the country road that led into the little town of Kirkwood five miles away. Maybe she had just gone in for supplies and been delayed. He shook his head. His attempts at rationalizing weren't doing him any good. No store would be open in town at the hour Ralph had seen her leave.

As he approached The Come and Get It Café, flashing police lights up the road caught his attention. He slowed and pulled over.

Alex pushed down the worry and sprinted across the road. The deputy standing beside the sheriff's car recognized him and waved.

"What's going on here?"

"Car went off the road in the early morning hours. I've got a rescue crew on the way. Night-shift deputy stopped a drunk driver up the way a piece. I suspect that driver ran this one off the road right before he got caught."

Alex stared down the steep ravine. Panic exploded inside him. Morgan's car was wedged against a tree facing downward. "That woman works for me. Do they know what her condition is?"

The deputy lifted his hat and rubbed his forehead. "I can't get down there. It's too steep. Got to wait for the rescue crew."

"How long has she been down there?"

"The drunk driver was picked up three miles up the road. That was a couple hours ago."

He couldn't wait for the rescue crew. Morgan might be injured or worse. Alex strode over to his truck and grabbed a length of rope he kept for catching horses. He tied the rope to a thin but sturdy tree.

"What are you doing?" The deputy stepped toward him.

Alex wrapped his calloused hands around the rope. "I've got to get down there and see if she's all right."

"Let the rescue crew take care of that," said the deputy.

Alex was already easing himself down the

incline. The rope was too short to get him right to the car. He'd have to free climb the remaining distance. He stepped backward until he came to the end of the rope. He let go of the rope after finding a foothold. He scrambled down to Morgan's car on the slanted ledge. Only the tree had stopped the car from rolling farther down the ravine. He ran over to the driver's door. His heart squeezed tight. Morgan's head pressed against the headrest. Her face showed no signs of life. He clicked open the door. The entire body of the car screeched. The tree, already bent from the force of the blow when the car hit it, would not hold much longer.

Morgan still had not moved. He feared the worst. Up above him, the rescue crew had arrived. They tied off rope as two of them prepared to bring down a stretcher.

He heard the cracking of the tree. She was going to slide down the mountain if he didn't do something. Adrenaline surged through him as he yanked open the door, reached across Morgan's lap and unbuckled her. Metal crunched and squeaked. The car started to tip forward. He gathered her into his arms and pulled her free just as the tree trunk snapped and the car rolled the remaining distance down the incline.

Morgan moaned and opened her eyes momentarily.

"Hey." He cupped her face in his hands as relief spread through him.

A faint smile crossed her lips before she slipped back into unconsciousness. His arms surrounded her and he held her close.

The two men on the rescue crew reached him. He helped them lift her into the hard-sided stretcher. She looked like a limp rag doll. They used pulleys to winch her up the mountain. One man operated the pulley and the other held on to the stretcher to keep it balanced. One of the rescuers tossed Alex a length of rope so he could get up the incline.

"I'm riding in the ambulance with her." His voice shook from exertion and fear. *Would she make it?*

He pulled himself back up to the road just as they were loading Morgan into the ambulance. The deputy reached down to help him up the remaining distance.

"How about we never pull a stunt like that again," said the deputy. His tone was gentle, but Alex knew he meant it.

Alex's attention was on Morgan being loaded into the ambulance. "She would have rolled the rest of the way down that hill if I hadn't gone down there."

"Kind of impulsive, wasn't it? Not like the Alex Reardon I know." The deputy studied him for a long moment. "You're more of a cautious kind of guy."

"The woman works for me. I was concerned for her safety. Sometimes caution is not in order." His voice faltered. The idea of losing her had upset him more than he wanted to admit.

The deputy nodded. "You'd better go be with her then."

The EMTs bent over Morgan as they took her vitals. One of them turned and waved Alex in. Alex sat beside Morgan as the ambulance gained speed. Her hands were folded over her stomach, and her eyes remained closed. His throat grew tight. In the moment when he'd looked through the window of her car and wasn't sure if she was dead or alive, he had realized he wanted her in his life in whatever capacity she was able to be.

The hospital in Kirkwood was a small, six-bed facility. The paramedics explained that if she had anything more serious than a concussion, they would airlift her into Des Moines.

A doctor and a nurse met them at the back door of the hospital and wheeled her in.

"Are you her husband?" the doctor asked.

Alex shook his head. "She works for me."

"You might want to notify her next of kin. I'm sure they'll want to be here."

He recalled the empty lines on her job application underneath the *In case of emergency* contact numbers. "She doesn't have any next of kin."

The nurse looked over her shoulder. "No next of kin? That's unheard of."

The doors swung shut, and he could only peer through the small window on the hospital room door as they worked on Morgan. Sadness for Morgan washed over him. There was no one he could call for her. She was completely alone in the world.

He slumped down in a chair. He made a call into Mrs. Stovall to let her know what had happened. It wasn't good for him to be away during their busy time, but he had a higher priority. When Morgan woke up, he wanted to make sure she at least had a friendly face to greet her. He couldn't change whatever had driven her to cut off all ties with the past, but he could at least be a support to her.

He shifted in the chair then rose to his feet and paced. From the time Morgan had gone missing to the time he thought she might be dead, a realization had grown inside him. He didn't want to lose her or drive her away. He wanted to help her in whatever way he could. In whatever way she would let him.

The nurse pushed through the doors and tore off her sterile gloves. "She's responsive. I think we're looking at a concussion, bruised ribs, scratches and abrasions. Rolling down a hill at high speeds like that, it could've been a lot worse."

"Thank you. Can I go in and see her?"

"Soon as she wakes up," said the nurse.

He sat spinning his hat in his hand for several minutes and then located a coffee machine. He had just finished his coffee when the nurse returned.

"She's coming around. The pain medication hasn't quite worn off but she could probably use some company. She's still a little shaken from the accident. Room 4."

Alex hurried down the hall. He found Morgan sitting up with her bed elevated as she rested her head against a pillow. Her face brightened when he entered the room.

"They said you got me out of the car just in time." Her voice was weak. She looked as though all vitality had been drained from her.

"The rescue crew was a little slow." Alex approached the bed. "Your car's a total. Sorry about that. You can borrow one of The Stables' vehicles until you can get another car."

She nodded. "Thank you for waiting to see me. It's nice to have a visitor." She seemed extremely fragile.

He pulled up a chair and sat close to her bed. "So what happened? Why were you on the road at that hour?"

She angled her head away from him. Although she hadn't given him an answer, he'd seen the suitcase in the car. She'd been planning to leave town. He remembered his earlier vow to take what she was willing to give. He didn't want her to leave. Maybe in time she would trust him with the truth. "How did the accident happen?"

She shook her head, still not looking at him. "Someone ran me off the road."

"The deputy said they picked up a drunk driver a couple miles up the road."

She turned back toward him. "Is that what it was?" Her words had a sharp edge to them as if she didn't believe what he said. "I'm not so sure." Her eyes glazed. In that single look, he realized there was a volume of information she wasn't sharing. He could see only the tip of the glacier where she was concerned.

Her hand trembled as she held on to the bed rail. He draped his hand over hers, and she didn't pull away. She looked up at him, her eyes drawing him in. His hand went up to her face. "Morgan, I just want you to know that… you can stay at The Stables as long as you want. I like having you there. I like the work you do." He had intended to say so much more. He wanted her to know that whatever she was running from, she could tell him.

She stared at the ceiling. The accident must have taken a toll on her emotionally. "I'm not sure I'll be able to pull my weight with these bruised ribs."

"We'll work it out. I want you to stay no matter what."

She studied him, her mouth turned up in a faint smile. "Thanks. That means a lot to me," she said.

He rose to his feet, twirling the cowboy hat in his hands. "You know, Morgan, I don't know what your whole story is." He paced, still twirling his hat as nervousness squeezed his chest tight. He had to get this out. He had to say it. "But if you're afraid of someone or hiding from someone, you can tell me. Is it a violent boyfriend or ex-husband? I'd understand about that."

Morgan stared at him for a long moment as though she were debating what to say. "You couldn't understand." Her voice filled with pain. She turned her head toward the pillow. "I'm really tired."

He stared at the back of her head. “Okay.” Feeling an overwhelming sense of defeat, he turned on his heels and left the room.

Morgan listened as Alex’s feet padded softly across the floor and the door closed. She opened her eyes and sat up, releasing a heavy breath and placing her hand on her chest. Chalk it up to the painkillers, but she had almost told him everything in the moment that he had assumed she was running from a crazy boyfriend. His kindness was unbearable in the face of her deception. And now he had offered to let her stay at The Stables even though she wouldn’t be able to do her job. She couldn’t do this to him.

A nurse came in with a tray of food. “Are you up to eating something?”

Morgan looked down at the steaming bowl of soup, the roll and the plate of Jell-O. “I’ll try. How long are they keeping me here?”

“Just overnight.” The nurse straightened her blankets so they covered her feet. “You can go home in the morning.”

Home. What a loaded word. She could never go home. Not as long as whoever was behind the baby snatching was still out there. And were The Stables even safe? The fire, the snake and now the car accident. It was all too much too fast to assume it was sheer coincidence.

The nurse stood back. "Ring that buzzer if you need anything. We'll be around in a couple of hours to check your vitals."

Morgan ate the bland meal, surprised at how hungry she was. So it looked like there was an explanation for her accident—a drunk driver. She closed her eyes, trying to remember some detail of the crash, but she couldn't even say what kind of car had hit her. And then as she thought about it, she wasn't even sure she had been hit. Maybe she'd veered off the road to avoid the other driver. The accident had happened so fast. She really didn't want to become known as the U.S. Marshals' problem child. But even they would have to admit that the mounting volume of accidents seemed suspicious. Maybe she would stick with her plan to leave The Stables, regardless of what the marshals said. This had become about more than just being safe. She needed to be somewhere she didn't have to keep looking into Alex's eyes and lying to him.

NINE

Alex sat in his office, staring at Morgan's job application. He had all the information in front of him to give to his detective friend—name, date of birth, Social Security number. He knew she'd been raised in Wyoming, loved working with children, was the most competent horse person he'd met in a long time and had deep-brown eyes that held a world of secrets. That was the sum total of what he knew about Morgan Smith. He set the application to one side and rested his elbows on his desk.

Even before he'd pulled the application, he knew he wouldn't call his detective friend. The idea had been driven by his frustration. As her employer, the scant information she'd given him was confidential. He realized he couldn't break the law, but the reasons ran even deeper than that. As much as he wanted to know who she was, he didn't want to give her a reason not to trust him. Snooping into her life would be a betrayal, even if she never found out. He wouldn't be able to live with himself.

He heard a rapping on his door, and Craig poked his head in. "I've got a bunch of guests who need help getting saddled up."

"I'll be right there." He pushed his chair back from the desk, glad to be abandoning paperwork for the better part of his job.

As he made his way across the grounds, he realized the day had stretched out to seem very long without Morgan here. But it wasn't just because she lightened his workload. True, she was an asset to The Stables, but her presence lightened his heart, too.

He wasn't sure why he still wanted to help her in whatever way she would let him. She'd closed down when he'd suggested she was running from an abusive boyfriend. When he'd seen her reaction, he again flirted with the idea that she was involved with something illegal and was on the run.

He just didn't want to believe that about her when so much of her character suggested otherwise. He hoped he wasn't setting himself up for betrayal. He couldn't go through that again.

* * *

Morgan was surprised when Serena Summers walked into her hospital room. The St. Louis office was at least a six-hour drive from Des Moines.

Serena explained. "When I called your cell this morning to ask you a question and got no answer I became concerned. Brendan hadn't heard from you either, so I called your boss telling him I was a friend from out of town. He told me about the accident and that you were here. I thought I should come up and see you."

"You called to ask a question? You mean you didn't get my message?"

A concerned look crossed Serena's expression. "No."

"I called last night and talked to a marshal. There was a fire yesterday, and someone was snooping around my house and later there was a snake in my bedroom."

"That message should have been passed on to me right away. Do you remember the name of the marshal you talked to?"

Morgan shook her head. "I didn't think to ask."

"This is serious." Serena narrowed her eyes as though she were thinking deeply.

Pain shot through Morgan's rib cage, and she winced.

Serena stepped closer to the bed, her voice filled with compassion. "How are you doing?"

"They're letting me go tomorrow. No broken bones or anything."

Serena studied her for a moment. "And how are you doing emotionally?"

Morgan's throat constricted. "I could be better."

"I have to ask. Where were you going that early in the morning?"

Morgan took a deep breath. "After finding the snake in my bedroom, I was afraid someone had put it there. I didn't feel safe."

"Given everything that happened I think we should look into this car accident. I know your boss thought it was a drunk driver."

Morgan stared at the ceiling. "Separately the incidents don't seem like anything, but together? Or maybe you think I'm paranoid because of what I've been through."

Serena shook her head. "I don't think you're paranoid. We should look into everything, but we shouldn't panic. Moving you is complicated and would take a while. We'd need clear confirmation that your cover was breached."

"What if they are trying to make my death

look like an accident because they don't want their fingerprints on this? You must be closing in on your investigation."

Serena stared at the wall as though she were mulling over what Morgan had said. "That is possible. I'm not dismissing your concerns, but we need something to work with."

"There was a man at the horse sale who seemed to be following me." Each breath Morgan took seemed to cause pain.

"That might be a place to start if you think you could identify him. You're in no condition to deal with a move anyway. I'm going to see if I can get one of our deputies set up as a guest where you work. That way we'll have someone watching you closely to ensure your safety until we can get to the bottom of this."

"Thank you for doing that." She dreaded going back to The Stables and facing Alex. But Serena was right—she wasn't in any condition to leave…not yet.

"Morgan, we're not going to leave you high and dry," Serena said. "I'll call you with the information about who we'll send for added protection as soon as I can set it up."

Morgan lifted her head off the pillow, which took every ounce of strength she had. She was more beat up than she wanted to admit. "I want to help any way I can. It would be good if Baby C could be reunited with her mom and any other babies that have been taken could be found. What was the question you called to ask me, anyway?"

"Since the other woman in the Mexico office has vaporized, we need to find some sort of connection back into the States. We have had linked incidents in Denver, Minneapolis and St. Louis that are tied to this ring. I assume you had to work with someone in the States to complete the adoptions. Do you remember who any of those people were?"

"Mostly I did the intake interviews of the moms. I didn't handle much of the adoption paperwork." She realized now that her duties had been restricted so she wouldn't get suspicious. "I did answer the phone if Marion was out, and I do remember taking a message from the States from a man named Dylan McIntyre. I don't know where the call came from." She smiled. "I remembered him because he seemed nice. He talked about his family."

Serena wrote down the name. "We'll see what we can do with that. Why don't you get some rest? I'll be in touch."

"I'm sorry for all the trouble I'm causing,"

Morgan said. "I didn't realize how hard this would be. I miss my family."

Serena closed her notebook. "I understand about the loneliness, but I want to remind you about how important it is that you don't form attachments, and not only because you risk revealing who you are."

"What do you mean?"

Serena took a moment to answer. "What these people do is horrifying. If they knew who you cared about, they might be able to gain your silence by threatening to hurt them."

Morgan sucked in a gasp of air that caused another blue-hot pain to sear through her. "I would never want someone I cared about to be hurt."

"I know that," Serena said. "What you know, what you can help us with, is part of a much bigger picture. Now get some rest." She waved as she shut the door.

Serena's shoes echoed down the hallway and then faded altogether. A few hours later, the nurse brought Morgan dinner. As the night wore on, she fell into a fitful sleep.

The next morning, Alex appeared in the doorway. "I'm here to take you home."

"Good, I'm ready to go." She managed to keep her voice neutral.

He lifted the plastic bag he held in his hand. “I hope it’s okay. I had one of the maids go over to your place and find you a change of clothes.”

His thoughtfulness was like a knife through her heart. “I could use those. I’m sure the ones I had on me are not fit to wear.” Maybe she couldn’t get in the car and drive away, but there were other ways to keep her distance. She didn’t want to see Alex hurt, and she didn’t want to lie to him anymore.

He placed the clothes on the end of her bed. “I’ll wait outside.”

Getting dressed took longer than Morgan had anticipated. She was bruised and sore and movement caused pain to rise up in new places. Finally, she stepped out into the hallway where Alex waited with a wheelchair. “Hospital regulation dictates you have to be pushed out. But they said I could do the honors.”

He pushed her slowly down the hospital hallway and through the automated doors to where his car was parked close to the curb. He opened the passenger door for her, and she eased herself down into the seat.

After returning the wheelchair, Alex got into the car and pulled out onto the road. The landscape clipped by as he spoke. “The doctor wants you up on your feet, but only very light activity."

"I'm sorry to do this to you. Even if I can't ride or lift a saddle, I can still feed and doctor the horses as needed." Morgan rested her head against the window. Now she was trapped in more ways than one. Her mobility was limited, too.

"We'll do all right, Morgan. Don't worry about it. Craig could probably use the money from picking up extra hours," Alex said.

How could he be so nice to her? Morgan stared out the window and remembered what Serena had said about giving the baby thieves bargaining chips. Anyone she loved or cared about would be in danger if the people behind all this found out about them. No matter what, she had to build a wall around her heart against Alex's kindness.

Alex drove right up to the door of Morgan's cottage. He hurried around to the passenger door. Though she worked hard to hide it, the tight line of her mouth told him she was in considerable pain. She tilted her head toward him, and he reached down to help her out of the low car.

Something had changed. She seemed even more guarded than usual. As he helped her to her porch, he could feel her pulling away from him emotionally. Maybe it was only the physical pain she was in that made her withdraw. He suspected it ran deeper.

He'd made a vow to be in her life in whatever capacity she allowed. Now he was seeing her retreat even more. He sensed his own heart closing off also. Having feelings for her only meant they'd be rebuffed. Hadn't he picked up on that pattern by now?

He could do the right thing—give her a place to stay while she mended and then let her do her job. He'd sign her paycheck and seek her advice on caring for the horses. He had to quit wearing his heart on his sleeve, hoping he could somehow win her over.

He placed a steadying hand on her back as she trudged up the stairs. He stepped ahead of her and pushed the door open. "You probably want to get a few hours' sleep."

She nodded. "Who would have thought you could get so tired from a car ride? I'll be well enough to come over and visit with the guests for lunch." She stepped into her living room, slowly scanning the expanse.

"Everything all right?"

"Yeah, sure." She offered him a stiff smile.

He saw that look in her eyes again and the subtle tightening of her mouth. Maybe coming back to the house where there'd been a poisonous snake brought back the frightening memory. "I'll leave you to it then."

She turned slowly to face him. "Thank you for doing this for me...for everything." She said the words as though she were reading them from a script.

He nodded and tipped his hat to her. "It's what I would do for anyone in your situation." He turned and stepped outside. As he passed by the window with the open curtain, he saw that she hadn't moved. He made his way back to the guesthouse, wondering why her thank you sounded more like a rejection.

TEN

The afternoon sun warmed the air as Morgan made her way across the grounds to the guesthouse. Craig stalked toward her from the parking lot where he'd been dropped off. The man in the old battered truck must be Craig's father, Robert.

As usual, Craig's eyebrows drew together in a scowl. She knew he wouldn't have a pleasant word for her even before he spoke.

"The horses are all fed and watered. When the kids come for the therapeutic riding class, I'll help you out as much as I can," she said.

Craig shook his hand in protest. "Let me guess—I'm going to have to saddle all the horses myself."

"Craig, I simply can't lift something that heavy yet," she said. "Besides, some of the clients like to saddle their own horses."

"Must be nice to be a princess." He walked away from her, muttering under his breath.

Morgan rolled her eyes. On any other day, she would have handled his snarky attitude just fine. But she was still in some pain even though it had been three days since the accident.

The marshal Serena had arranged for her protection came out of the guesthouse and walked toward her. Burke Trier had first arrived three days ago, when she'd just gotten home and was still spending much of her day in the cottage. But anytime she was outside, Burke showed up.

Burke walked past her and tipped his hat. "Morning, Miss Smith. Getting ready to teach your lesson?"

"As much as I can. I'm still moving kind of slowly."

Burke had checked into the guesthouse under the guise of wanting to have a long-term ranch experience. He was a tall, lean man with dark hair and a dimple in his chin.

Burke leaned a little closer and lowered his voice. "Everything still looking all clear for you?"

Morgan nodded.

Alex came around the corner of the guesthouse and she and Burke broke up their conversation. As Alex approached, she saw the dark circles under his eyes and the drawn expression. A pang of guilt shot through her. Craig may have picked up some of the slack, but clearly Alex was doing the work of two people.

The first of the students for the class was already pulling into the parking lot.

"Thought I'd help out with the class as much as I could," Morgan said. "Craig is already headed toward the barn to get the horses saddled up for the kids who can't do it themselves."

"I'd better get down there and give him a hand."

"You can probably talk Burke into helping since he wants all that authentic experience." She grabbed his arm. "Hey, maybe we should let Craig help out with the class, too."

Alex raised his eyebrows. "Craig doesn't exactly have good people skills."

"Neither do some of those kids. They might end up being two peas in a pod." She glanced over at the parking lot, where several other cars had pulled up. "Why don't you try pairing him with Richie? His mom, Adele, mentioned that she's not going to be able to come for a couple of weeks this month. This would be a good chance to see if Craig could handle the responsibility."

Alex shrugged. "We'll give it a shot."

Morgan greeted the clients. When Richie and his mom arrived, she explained about his working with Craig and led them down to the corral where Craig had just turned a horse over to a young boy and his aide.

"Craig, this is Richie and his mom, Adele." Morgan touched Richie's shoulder.

Adele stepped forward. "I've got extra work at my accounting firm for the next couple of weeks because of tax season so I can't stay. Morgan said you might be able to help out so Richie can continue his lesson. He looks forward to them."

"Me?" The look on Craig's face bordered somewhere between shock and fear.

Morgan tensed. Maybe this had been a mistake. She'd thought asking Craig in front of the clients would prevent his usual outburst. "Alex and I both think you are ready to handle more responsibility."

The harsh angles of Craig's expression melted. "Really." He raised his chin and squared his shoulders. "Course I can." Craig stepped toward Richie. "Why don't you come on over with me?"

Richie responded by turning sideways and staring at the ground.

Morgan glanced at Adele, both of them ready to explain Richie's personality. Morgan opened her mouth to speak but then watched as Craig's posture relaxed and his voice softened. "Or, how about I bring the horse over to you?"

Richie raised his head and nodded enthusiastically.

She'd known all along that Craig was sensitive to the animals, but this was the first time she'd seen him show an awareness of another person's needs. Maybe if Craig's confidence was built up through accomplishing new things, he'd let go of his resentment toward her.

From across the corral, she saw Alex observing the interaction. He gave her a thumbs-up sign.

Adele stared out at the kids as their aides led them around the arena or out for short trail rides. "The work you do here is so important."

Morgan nodded. "I suppose that's true." Though she hid her reaction from Adele, the comment stirred up sadness in her. She had thought the work she was doing in Mexico was important, too.

Her cell phone rang, and she stepped away from Adele. She didn't need to look at the number to know that it was one of the St.

Louis marshals calling her. Alex was the only other person who knew her number. "Hello."

"Morgan. Serena here. I've arranged for a sketch artist to sit down with you since you said you thought you could identify the man you saw at the horse sale."

"Thank you for doing this," Morgan said.

"If you can, we'll have something solid to work with."

Morgan's spirits lifted. Maybe they could get this thing resolved. "I understand."

"When would you like him to come out?

Morgan tensed as her gaze traveled to where Alex had stepped in to calm a jumpy horse. "I don't want him to come out here. I don't like having to make up stories to my boss. Can I meet him in Des Moines?"

"Sure. There's a café not too far from the Botanical Gardens that's easy to find. I'll send a picture to your phone so you know what he looks like, along with his name and directions to the gardens," Serena said. "Marshal Trier can go with you if you want."

They settled on a time and Morgan hung up. One of the horses had planted her feet and refused to move despite the aide tugging on the reins.

Morgan stepped in. "Don't keep pulling. She'll get agitated." She stared up at the nine-year-old girl on the horse who was talking in sign language.

The aide signed back and then addressed her comment to Morgan. "She wants to get moving."

"Let me take over for a while. Jojo can be kind of stubborn sometimes." Morgan made a clicking sound with her tongue. The horse plodded forward.

She could see Richie and Craig seemed to be getting along quite well. Burke leaned against the fence not too far from her. She caught a glimpse of Alex as he worked his way around the arena. The sun shining on his hair brought out the coppery highlights. He locked gazes with her for a moment. Her heart fluttered.

Maybe the guy she'd seen at the horse sale was the one responsible for all the other trouble. If they caught him, would she be able to stay in this place she was growing to love? Morgan turned away. No matter what, she'd never be able to tell Alex who she really was.

She wasn't looking forward to asking Alex if she could borrow a car. Hopefully he wouldn't ask too many questions.

Alex watched Morgan come out of her cottage as he rode a young palomino toward the open door of the stable. The trail ride had done him good after a long day of work. With Morgan not able to ride yet, he liked having an excuse to get some additional time on the horses. He hadn't minded the extra work, but feeling like there was a wedge between him and Morgan was wearing on him.

Just outside the stables, he tightened the reins. "Whoa." He dismounted. Morgan was headed toward the stable with a look of determination. Burke, who was riding his horse around the arena, slowed down some. The guy sure showed a keen interest in Morgan. He kicked himself mentally for the surge of jealousy he felt. Just more evidence that he still had feelings for her. He clenched his jaw. They were feelings that would never go anywhere or lead to anything.

He braced himself as Morgan drew close. Whatever she had to say to him, he was not going to read into it or become hopeful that she would open up to him. She'd seemed more closed down than ever since the accident.

The horse's hooves made clopping sounds on the hard ground as he led the mare toward her stall.

"I saw you coming in from your ride." Her voice pelted his back like a soft summer rain.

"Yup." Alex pulled the saddle off the horse.

She stepped toward the horse and slipped off her bridle. "I haven't had a chance to ask you—do you mind if I borrow that car? I need to go into the city."

A simple enough request. He could handle that. "Sure, when did you need it?"

"Tomorrow. I'm meeting a friend around two o'clock. I'll make sure all the horses are fed before I leave."

"Tomorrow? How fortunate. I have a meeting with the owners of The Stables around that time. I can drive you in."

Veiled panic, quivering lips and nervous sideways glances told him that she didn't like the idea. He tensed. Now she didn't even want to ride in a car with him.

"I…I suppose that would work. I'm not sure how long this meeting will take."

"Meeting? I thought you said you were getting together with a friend." Why did she have to be evasive? The level of frustration he felt kicked up a notch. Not wanting her to be the target of his ire, he turned his back and stomped toward the feed bin.

You can trust me, Morgan. Whatever your secret is, you can trust me.

He loaded the bucket with feed. The silence was so intense, he wondered if she'd left. When he looked back toward the stall, she still stood watching him, her hand idly stroking the palomino's nose.

"Driving might not be the best thing for you, Morgan, considering you're still healing up," he said.

She thought for a moment. "I suppose you're right," she said. "Does eleven-thirty sound good? Gives us plenty of time if the traffic is heavy."

He stalked toward the horse stall and poured in the feed. His arm brushed over hers as he bent to dump the feed. She took a step back but remained close to the horse.

He straightened and rested the bucket on the top rail of the stall gate. "That sounds like it will work to me." His words had come out harsher than he'd intended.

He thought he detected hurt in her eyes. He shook his head as she turned her back and left the stables. They couldn't keep playing this game. He'd been lying to himself when he thought he could draw the boundary at working together. His attraction to her was too intense to keep his feelings at bay. But every time he reached out to her in even the smallest way, she found a way to put up another wall.

Yet, she had gotten extremely cozy with

Burke in short order. He was starting to think he'd read the signals all wrong. She really didn't like him at all.

Though the drive to Des Moines took over two hours, Morgan managed to keep the conversation focused on the horses, clients and other things related to The Stables. She had texted Burke that he didn't need to drive her since she would be either with Alex or the forensic artist. That meant she didn't have one more odd thing to explain to Alex. Burke texted her back and said to be on the safe side he would follow in his car. As they talked, Alex's voice and expressions became animated. She loved how passionate he was about his work.

"I think you found your true calling. Good thing you didn't stay in that room with no windows," she said.

Alex smiled. "I agree. What about you? Do you feel like you found your calling?"

Morgan's heart squeezed tight. She let out a heavy breath. She'd thought she'd found her calling in Mexico. "I'm not sure."

"I don't know you that well, but I'd say that your work at The Stables with those kids comes close." His tone held a note of affection.

She was having a hard time receiving the

compliment. Everything she was doing at The Stables was based on a lie. How could it be her calling? If things went well with the forensic artist today, they might catch the guy who had followed her at the horse sale. Maybe he was the same man responsible for the other things that had happened. There hadn't been any accidents since Burke had been put on duty.

The drive into the city and their conversation had been so comfortable. It was the first time they'd spent any time together since the car accident. It was easy to relax around Alex. She could feel her guard going down. "Things aren't always what they seem."

Alex stopped at a red light. His expression gave away that he was confused. "What are you talking about?"

She had said too much already, opened the door too wide. Morgan stared out at the street ahead. Time to change the subject. "So what's your meeting about?" she asked.

"There is another horse-boarding business in the area and another one being built. The owners want to strategize how we can step up our game in terms of customer service and promotion to remain competitive."

"Sounds interesting," she said.

"Who are you meeting at the café?"

"Just a friend." She turned her head toward the window so he wouldn't look into her eyes. It was so easy to tread into dangerous water with him. "I think I'm only a few blocks away from where you can let me out."

"Okay, Morgan." His words held an undercurrent of weariness.

He pulled into a parking space in front of the café.

She couldn't bring herself to look him in the eye. All he'd done was ask a simple question after he had graciously answered hers. She hated doing this to him. "I'll call when I'm done." She slammed the door and raced up the steps to the café.

Still trying to shake off how upset evading Alex made her, she gave her name to the hostess, who pointed out a table where a man sat with a laptop and sketch pad. The man stood up as she approached. "Morgan?"

"Yes."

He held out his hand. "I'm Keith Miller. Our time is limited so we should probably get started. If you want to take a seat, I've got the identification software all fired up."

She scooted into the booth and Keith sat down beside her. "What's the sketch pad for?"

"Sometimes if the software isn't giving us helpful options, it's easier to do things the old-fashioned way." He placed his hands on the keyboard. "So why don't we start with what you remember about this man?"

Morgan thought for a moment. "The thing I remember is that he was bulky, wide through the chest like a football player or boxer."

Keith nodded. "What can you tell me about his facial features?"

Morgan closed her eyes. The horse sale seemed like ages ago. Despite the scare, she'd had a good day because she'd been with Alex. She'd seen his passion for the horses and been attracted to how protective he was of her.

"Miss Smith?"

"Oh, sorry." She closed her eyes, trying to recall what the man had looked like. "He had a baseball cap pulled low on his face.... I do remember his eyes."

After working for nearly an hour, Morgan felt frustrated. She hadn't seen the man long enough to come up with anything substantial. The face they'd managed to put together was vague at best. "I know if I saw him again, I would recognize him. It's really hard to pull things out of thin air."

Keith offered some sympathetic comments as he closed out his program. "Maybe we can revisit this if details come back to you."

"But I really haven't given you enough to

work with, have I?" The hope she had started the day with shrank.

Keith shook his head. "We'll try again. Maybe something will come back to you."

As she watched Keith leave the café, despair clouded her mind. Any possibility that she could come up with something solid for the marshals was dashed. Morgan paid for her coffee and headed out to the street to walk off her frustration. After a few blocks she called Alex and let him know she'd be waiting on a bench outside the gardens. His response was short and to the point. Maybe his meeting with the owners hadn't gone well, and maybe he was still mad about how she'd treated him.

The café and Botanical Gardens were close to trails that looked out on a river. She made her way toward a park bench that allowed her a view of the street so she could see Alex coming. She sat down, still upset over not being able to ID that man she'd seen at the horse sale.

A strange car with dark windows eased by her on the street. She didn't become alarmed until the car did a U-turn in the parking lot and passed by her a second time. She'd let her guard down. She shouldn't be alone. Morgan shot to her feet and started walking back toward the gardens where the crowds were. She breathed a sigh of relief when she saw Deputy Trier's car parked by the curb.

Alex hung up the phone and pulled into traffic. His conversation with Morgan had been icy. He didn't want to give away how upset he was. The car ride had been their first chance to spend time together since the accident. And she had been just as cold as ever to him.

Jealousy sparked through him every time he saw her with Burke. The heat of the emotion surprised him. He didn't have any sort of claim on her. All through his meeting, he'd been distracted, unable to deny the strong feelings he had for her. Stuffing them down wasn't working. He hated himself for the jealousy. The other side of envy was affection. Despite all his efforts, he couldn't stop caring about her. No amount of denial or pushing away of emotion would change that.

He pressed the brake as the light in front of him turned red. He was still about ten minutes away from her, assuming that traffic wouldn't get any worse. Alex tapped his fingers on the steering wheel, then eased forward when the light changed.

How had she managed to get under his skin anyway, as closed off as she was? He found a parking space close to where she said she would be. The bench where she was supposed to be waiting was empty. Alex pushed open the car door and strode toward the trails and river. He walked the grounds around the bench and scanned along the riverfront. No Morgan.

He tried her cell phone.

"Hello?" Her voice sounded shaky.

"Morgan, are you all right?"

"Alex, you got here fast. I...decided to go for a walk. I'm on that busy corner across from the gardens."

"There's parking by the gardens, so why don't you meet me there?" He hung up, found a parking space and made his way toward the street corner, wondering what had upset Morgan so much.

ELEVEN

As she stood on the busy corner waiting to cross, Morgan tried not to dwell on how discouraging the day had been. The car that had gone past her twice had not been a threat. But the incident was a reminder of how she could never let her guard down. She wanted all this to be over, to get back to a normal life. She tried to picture a time when this would all be behind her. Would she be able to get married, have children, see her family?

She stared across the busy street, willing the walk sign to come on. Traffic zoomed by. The light changed and she stepped out into the street. A car barreled toward her. Her vision filled with a blur of color as tires squealed and horns honked.

Arms wrapped around her, yanked her toward the curb and spun her around. Alex pulled her close. Her heart pounded out a wild rhythm. Around her, she could hear drivers shouting as traffic resumed. Her hand rested on his chest.

"Oh, dear, you were nearly killed." An older woman put her hand over her mouth. "That driver ran the light." The woman gazed at Alex. "It's a good thing we have brave young men like you who can run the hundred-yard dash in three seconds flat."

Alex laughed. "I don't think I was quite that far away."

Morgan relished the warmth of Alex's arms around her. "Thank you—that was quite a rescue." She winced as pain sliced through her rib cage.

He gazed down at her as people maneuvered around them on the street. "You all right?"

"Just a reminder that I haven't totally healed." She couldn't stop trembling. "Guess I was so lost in thought I wasn't paying attention."

"You're still a little shaken up. You want to sit down? Catch your breath." Alex glanced around and then pointed toward the Botanical Gardens. "It's restful in there."

"That would be nice." Her voice gave away how upset she was. As they walked up to the entrance, she was grateful for the calming effect of Alex's hand on her back.

The gardens were in a geodesic dome with a huge sculpture at the entrance, half circles of metal in rainbow colors. They paid the fee and entered. An abundance of tropical plants interspersed with waterfalls and bridges and walkways greeted them. She eased down onto a bench in a secluded spot.

Alex sat beside her. "That guy nearly ran you over. Crazy city drivers, huh?"

She nodded, wishing that she could believe it was only an inattentive driver. She hadn't noticed anyone following her. Would this ever be over? Right now it felt like there would never be a time when she didn't have to be on her guard.

A waterfall hummed in the background as people's voices echoed off the dome. The events of the day weakened her emotional resolve. "It's beautiful here, isn't?"

"I've always liked it."

When she looked at Alex she knew she was falling apart. Being in this romantic place and peering into his eyes only reminded her of what she didn't have. What she couldn't have. Her eyes rimmed with moisture.

"Hey." Alex's voice was filled with compassion. "You're safe now." He reached over and wiped the tear from her cheek. "It was just some bad driver trying to get someplace ten seconds faster."

He leaned close, and she breathed in the soapy clean of his skin. His hand rested on her cheek. He looked into her eyes. The affection she saw there was heartbreaking.

"You don't need to be afraid." His voice had become husky.

How she wanted that to be true. His gaze held a magnetic pull. She could not look away. Her longing for him intensified. If only... Tears flowed down her cheek.

He leaned in as though he were going to kiss her but stopped. "Maybe I'm out of line."

She shook her head, not understanding.

"You and Burke."

She laughed. "There's nothing between us." She looked at the ground.

"In that case." He placed his finger under her chin, tilted her head up and kissed her. She melted beneath his touch as his mouth covered hers. His arms surrounded her, pulling her close. She responded to the strength and warmth of his kiss. In his arms she felt released from the pain and uncertainty of her life. She'd wanted this for a long time.

His arm wrapped around her waist. His stubble grazed her smooth cheek as he deepened the kiss. His hand brushed through her hair and touched her ear. She couldn't pull away if she'd wanted to. He kissed her lightly several more times before tilting his head back.

Breathless, she opened her eyes.

"Guess I don't like to see you cry." The look in his eyes made her skin tingle.

Even as she basked in the afterglow of his kiss, she knew it had been a mistake. He had accepted her completely. He hadn't demanded answers from her. She could give him nothing in return. Any romance between them was doomed.

His face remained close to hers, his eyes searching. "That was quite a kiss. I hope there's more," he said.

She scooted away. His proximity was enticing. Her mind told her it was cruel to both of them to set up any expectation for romantic involvement, but her heart only wanted him to hold her. Shc pulled the words from the pit of her stomach. "I can't."

His expression clouded with disappointment. "But I thought..."

"I can't be in a relationship right now." Even as the words spilled out, the heat of his touch, the way her lips had yielded to him, lingered.

He let out a heavy breath. "Whatever you

want, Morgan." His words tinged with anger as he shot to his feet.

Morgan crumpled inside. She'd hurt him. "It wasn't a bad kiss, though," she said with a small smile.

He sat back down, his voice softening. "No, not at all."

His hand rested on the bench. She could feel her own hand magnetically drawn to it. She crossed her arms.

Don't mess it up by sending him mixed signals.

Alex stood up. "Let's get back to The Stables where things make a little more sense, shall we? We've got that overnight trail ride coming up in a couple of weeks. I think we should start planning right away."

So they were back to talking about work as though nothing had happened. That's the way it had to be.

Morgan followed. As they moved through the lush green plants past scented flowers, she knew the kiss would be impossible to forget.

Alex awoke to the buzzing of the door. It was nearly 2:00 a.m. That could mean only one thing: There was some emergency with the horses. He shoved on his boots and shirt and hurried from his private quarters through the lobby of the guesthouse.

Morgan stood on the porch. Her hair was loose, and it looked like she'd slipped her jeans on over her pajamas. "The horses got out of that pasture where we put them to graze. The gate must not have been latched right."

It had been weeks since the car accident. Morgan had healed enough to start riding again. She spent much of her time scouting trails for the overnight camping trip, and he had confined himself to the office as much as he could. Alex found himself thinking about their kiss more often than he wanted to admit. Confusion clouded his thoughts. He had seen desire in her eyes right before he kissed her. Why, then, had she denied she had those feelings?

"Craig was supposed to fix the latch on that gatc." He walked over to grab his jacket off the hook.

Morgan followed him into the coat room. "You've been keeping Craig pretty busy lately. Maybe he didn't have time to get to it."

Craig seemed to be becoming a bigger and bigger point of contention between them. Alex knew their fights weren't really about Craig. The subtext of all their disagreement was his frustration over his unrequited affection.

Pushing aside his ire, he placed his hat on his head and tried to come up with a plan for getting the horses in. "So we don't have any horses we can ride to catch the others?"

"Chipper's Boy came right up to the cottage. He wanted to be caught." Morgan still had not calmed down.

"He's a good horse." Alex's mind raced. "I'll get the two-way radios. There should be some flashlights in the utility shed."

They met up a few minutes later by the corral. Several of the horses hung close to the perimeter. They could be led in easily enough. It was the horses running across property lines and ending up hurt that concerned him.

Morgan had already saddled Chipper's Boy.

"Let's get the easy ones in first. Then I'll take the truck out on the road. You can work the trails with Chipper. Let me know when you spot one. Are you any good at lassoing?"

"I can handle it," Morgan said.

"Let's get this done." He'd missed being around her, working closely with her, but avoidance seemed the best strategy because his attraction to her held sway over his ability to think straight. She couldn't have been any clearer than she had been at the gardens. He had to accept that there could be nothing between them.

In all, twelve of the horses were easily led back into their stalls. That meant four more were unaccounted for. Alex drove out into the trail area. He could see Morgan's light in the distance. He searched the landscape. They had to get the horses in. This could end up costing money, and it was a huge safety risk to the horses. If one of the boarded horses ended up injured, The Stables' reputation was on the line. With two other stables in the area stepping up their game, he didn't need the bad PR something like this would generate. The fire had already caused him to lose some clients.

Static noises came across his radio and then he heard Morgan's voice. "I got one over here. I'll lead him over and we can tie him up behind the truck."

After a few hours of searching, they'd located all the horses but Bluebell. Morgan tethered the last horse to the back of Alex's truck. "I'm going to keep looking for Bluebell if you want to take those guys in."

"I can do that, but I'll come back out and give you a hand," Alex offered.

Of all the horses, losing Bluebell held the

most dire consequences. Stephanie Bliss was not an easy client to deal with. Bluebell was an extremely valuable horse. Plus theft could be an issue if someone dishonest found the horse.

His frustration rose back to the surface. "Did you see if Craig fixed that latch?"

Morgan tied off the rope with a jerking motion. "I don't know one way or the other. Could we not point the finger at that kid?"

"Why do you keep defending him? He's not even nice to you." His words came out angrier than he had intended. Before his words were even out, he knew he wasn't really angry about Craig. This was about her rejection of him.

"I see goodness in him. His kindness toward the animals tells me that." She stepped toward him. Her face was only a few inches from his. "It's just going to take time for him to trust me."

Alex chortled. He could say the same thing about his relationship with her. But all his efforts had been blown out of the water by her pushing him away. "That doesn't work. Believe me."

She placed her hands on her hips. "Can we not have this argument right now? We have a horse to find." She stomped back toward her horse. She stuck her leg in the stirrup and swung on. He listened to the sound of the fading hoof steps before climbing into the cab of his truck.

Clearly, there was too much tension between them and the only thing that kept it at bay was not working in close quarters. He pounded his fist on the steering wheel. She made him so crazy.

She wasn't willing to share anything about her past. Yet she hadn't pulled away from the kiss. She had liked it as much as he had. So why had she shut down the possibility of a relationship? He let out a heavy breath. Even with everything she had done, he could not let go of the idea that she was a good person.

That was one thing they had in common. She had a blind spot where Craig was concerned, and he wanted to believe in her despite all the evidence to the contrary.

He drove slowly as the horses lumbered behind the truck. If maintaining their distance was the only thing that kept them from being at each other's throats, the camping trip was going to be a nightmare.

Morgan slowed her horse and searched for Bluebell. The land was open and flat with minimal tree cover. But a black horse against a black background wouldn't be easy to spot.

After weeks without an incident, Deputy Trier had been called off duty. It had been three days since he'd left, and everything had remained calm. She still wasn't so sure. It was hard to let go of her suspicions and now things with Alex were only getting worse.

Her insides felt like they'd been stirred with a hot poker. She hadn't meant to get into a fight with Alex. How ironic would it be if the conflict with Alex was what finally led to her relocation? She doubted the Witness Security Program would invest time and money just because she couldn't get along with her boss.

Even now as she searched for Bluebell, she wished Alex was out here with her.

Every time she stood close to Alex, she remembered their kiss. She hated pushing him away. She hated the lies. Why couldn't things be different?

She didn't like the way Craig had become the rope in the emotional tug of war she was having with Alex. She really wanted that kid to have a chance, and she'd seen some progress. As Craig shared more with her, she was beginning to see that his anger was a defense mechanism. He was afraid to let people close.

Morgan halted her horse and shone the

flashlight in a broad circle. Trees formed jagged dark shapes. The quiet was disconcerting. She didn't like being out here alone. Now she regretted her fight with Alex even more. Would he come back out and help her as promised?

She rode onward, tuned in to the sounds around her and shining the flashlight in front of her. The trail ended and she came out on a country road. She could see the lights of a neighboring farm but no sign of Bluebell anywhere.

Her horse's hooves clopped along the road. Dogs barked as she approached the farm. A porch light came on and a man stepped out.

"What do you want?" Clearly, the man didn't like being awakened in the night.

"Sorry to bother you," she shouted. "I'm looking for a runaway horse."

The man shouted back, "I haven't seen anything like that. Kind of late, isn't it?"

The man's no-nonsense style of conversation reminded her of her own father. She waved at the man and rode on. Though she'd taken the path where the horse had most likely run, Bluebell could be on the other side of the county by now. She rode for another twenty minutes. When she passed a field, movement in her peripheral vision caught her attention.

Moonlight washing over the landscape revealed Bluebell standing in a grove of trees.

Morgan shook her head. "You are such a pain." She dismounted Chipper's Boy, pulled her rope from the saddle and approached the horse. As she drew near, the horse seemed undisturbed by her presence. She moved in a little closer. Bluebell lifted her head but didn't bolt.

Morgan slipped the rope easily over the horse's head. She stroked her neck. "No fight or anything. You just got tired of running, didn't you? You're ready to go home. That makes two of us."

She led the horse down the road and back through the fields. She called in on the radio. "Alex, I found her and I'm bringing her in."

The line opened up. "That sounds good, Morgan. Why don't you try to get a few hours of sleep?" His voice was soft, filled with either regret or fatigue. "Tomorrow is going to be busy with that trail ride."

"Roger that." She clicked off her radio and steered the horses toward home. Out here in the open fields with the stars above her, she felt a profound sense of loneliness.

She had recovered from the car accident. She was stronger now. The truth was, she didn't want to leave The Stables. Even though interacting with Alex had gotten tricky, she didn't want to lose the children or the horses. She'd fallen in love with this place.

Bluebell whinnied behind her.

She and Bluebell had something in common. They were both tired of running and wanted a place to call home.

The lights of The Stables came into view. She half expected to see Alex standing by his truck waiting for her, but the place looked completely abandoned. He must've gone back to the guesthouse already.

She should be relieved that he was choosing to keep his distance. In theory it made staying here that much easier. But as she looked out at the empty corrals and the single light on in the guesthouse, all she felt was loss.

TWELVE

Morgan cast an anxious glance toward The Stables' parking lot. Though it had filled up quickly with people coming to load their horses for the overnight trail ride, she saw no sign of Craig. He'd been indifferent when she'd invited him to go. Maybe he wouldn't show.

As she loaded the final therapy horse into the trailer, she had to be honest about the disappointment she felt with Craig not showing up.

Alex came around the side of the trailer. "I think we'll be ready to move out of here in about ten minutes."

Morgan nodded with a final glance toward the parking lot.

Alex stood beside her. "You had to know he wouldn't take you up on the offer."

"I keep seeing these little glimmers in Craig that tell me a turnaround is possible."

His expression hardened. "You can't win everyone over, Morgan. Sometimes you have to give up on people."

His words stung. Is that what he thought about her? That he had tried to win her over and failed? Even the most minor disagreement between them cut deep, and Craig was a growing point of contention.

Alex leaned a little closer to her, his eyes blazing. "Kindness does not win people over."

She picked up the challenging tone of his voice. The intensity of his gaze demanded an explanation she could not give. "I can still hope."

Looking for an excuse to get away, Morgan made her way back to the guesthouse to see if Mrs. Stovall needed help loading the chuck wagon.

The sound of screeching brakes drew her attention to the parking lot. Craig's father sat behind the wheel of the truck, and Craig jumped out with his father on his heels.

"Hey, boy!" The older man grabbed his son by the shoulder and swung him around.

Morgan raced toward the parking lot. The clumsiness of the man's actions had set off alarm bells for her—Robert had been drinking.

"Get your hands off me," Craig shouted.

Morgan struggled to keep her voice casual. "Hey, Mr. Jones. So glad you brought Craig."

Robert Jones swayed and offered her a glassy-eyed stare.

She didn't want him getting back in that truck. Not in his condition. "I think Mrs. Stovall has a pot of coffee on in the guesthouse. Why don't you stay awhile?"

Robert pointed a shaky finger at her. "You stay out of this. You're the reason I'm not working."

"Dad." Craig's face turned red with embarrassment.

"You shut up, boy." He leaned toward Craig, swaying slightly. "You disrespect me."

Craig shook his head and took a step back.

Robert lunged at him and shook his son's shoulders roughly. "Show some respect."

"Please, Mr. Jones. I think it would be best if you stepped away." Morgan placed her hand on Robert's forearm, squeezed it and tried to lift it off Craig's shoulder.

Robert whirled around, all his rage suddenly focused on Morgan. "You." His hands clenched into fists.

Craig took several steps back and then ran.

Morgan's heart pounded when Robert raised his arm as though to hit her.

Alex was suddenly between them, grabbing Robert's hands. "I think you'd better back off right now."

Robert took a swing at Alex, but Alex backed out of the way. He gripped Robert's shoulders. "Step away now."

The force of Alex's voice seemed to quell the man's anger. Alex cupped his shoulders and turned him toward the guesthouse. "Why don't you sit for a minute? We'll get someone to give you a ride home." He led the man away without so much as a backward glance toward Morgan.

Morgan's heart raced from nearly having been Robert's punching bag. Alex must have been watching the interaction, ready to jump in. Even after all she'd done to him, his decency always rose to the surface. It only made her like him more.

She looked around. Most people were busy with packing. Craig was nowhere in sight. The kid had clearly been embarrassed by his father's behavior. He was only a teenager, but no male liked a woman stepping in to defend him against another man. Would he change his mind about going?

She busied herself with the final bit of loading, all the while seeing no sign of Craig or Alex. She got into the cab of the truck she'd been assigned to drive to the trailhead.

Richie and his mom came up to her. "Alex said there is space in your cab for us to ride."

"Yeah, sure. Hop in."

Morgan got behind the wheel. When she peered into the side-view mirror, she saw Craig getting into the truck that would serve as the chuck wagon.

She breathed a sigh of relief. At least he was coming, but she had no idea what sort of emotional condition he was in. She feared that the incident would make him even more standoffish to her because of the shame he felt about his dad. Teenagers embarrassed easily, and this altercation had been over the top.

She watched Alex climb into his truck and pull out onto the road. Their relationship had started to feel like a rubber band that had been twisted to the breaking point. Would being in close quarters for two days be the thing that finally made them snap?

Alex pulled into the flat area that served as the trailhead. Morgan's truck along with several others followed behind.

He'd gotten Craig's father a ride home. How long would it be, though, until there was another incident? He couldn't blame the son for the father's actions, but at the same time he didn't want an environment where his guests were unsafe.

Morgan jumped out of her cab and opened the trailer gate to back a horse out. When he had thought Robert was going to hit Morgan, his instinct to protect her had kicked into high gear.

The thought of anyone harming her in any way incensed him. He shook his head. Even though there had been tension between them, he could not cut her out of his emotional landscape.

As he worked to get horses unloaded and riders secured, he noticed some guests he didn't recognize. Some people had brought friends or family, and he'd honored any request for an extra horse that came in.

He watched Craig help several of the students from the class get on their horses. Morgan had made progress with him where his interactions with others were concerned. He had to give her credit for that.

When everyone was settled on their horses, Morgan took the lead on the trail and the others fell in behind her. After riding up and down the line to make sure all the riders were comfortable, Alex moved toward the rear. Mrs. Stovall drove the truck and trailer that held the food and other supplies.

As they rounded a bend, Alex glanced over his shoulder. Another truck and trailer had pulled into the parking area. Not one of theirs. All the guests were accounted for. Probably someone out for a day ride.

After a few hours, they stopped by a river to let the horses drink and rest. Multiple complaints of sore bottoms arose as people dismounted. He saw Morgan coming toward him through the throng of horses and people. Hopefully, she only had some sort of logistical thing that needed to be handled.

He swung around to the other side of his horse and checked the tightness of the straps. "What is it?"

"I wanted to thank you for...earlier today. For stepping in like you did."

"You're a valuable asset to this place. I wouldn't want to see you injured again." He regretted his words even before he saw the hurt in her eyes. She was way more than an asset.

"I'm grateful. That's all." She lowered her head and walked away.

Alex clenched his teeth. He didn't need to be that cold to her. The line between attraction and anger was a thin one. Love spurned led to hostility.

They rode on through the day, stopping

for lunch and rest until they came to the spot Morgan had picked out for them to camp. Mrs. Stovall and her staff produced a hearty meal of beans, steak and rolls, some of which they'd cooked over the open fire. As the light faded, several of the riders retrieved guitars from the chuck wagon truck to play.

Alex walked the perimeter of the camp. Music and laughter came from around the campfire.

His regret over his harsh words to Morgan ate at his gut. He'd have to do something about that. Something he should have done a long time ago. He could be honest with her about why her withholding information bothered him so much.

He stared out on the horizon, praying that he would find the courage he needed.

Off in the distance, he noticed a light bouncing along. So they weren't out here alone. It was not totally unexpected; they were on public land. Still, he wondered what a lone rider was doing traveling through the darkness.

As it grew dark, Morgan poured out the final bit of feed for the horses. They didn't need much because there was plenty of grass for them to graze on. She held her flashlight in her teeth. The tiki torches that had been set up around the camp were too far away to provide much illumination. Most of the campers had retreated to their tents, though the strumming of a guitar and soft laughter told her that some of the night owls were still up visiting.

She'd grabbed Craig to help her out. He kept his distance, not saying anything to her and choosing to feed from the opposite direction she had started in. Her hopes of the trail ride turning their relationship around seemed dashed. She could only guess at how he was feeling. Shame over the incident with his father must have driven a wedge between them. Morgan wove in and out of the horses, checking for saddle sores or any other injury that needed to be dealt with.

Craig slowly worked his way back to her. Now only a couple of horses were between them. She took that as a sign that he was ready to talk.

She rested her arm on the horse's back. "Nice night out here, huh?"

"It's all right I guess," he blurted, sounding a little defensive.

She allowed for a short silence to fall between them while she checked one of the horse's hooves.

"I'm sorry about what happened this morning," she kept her response soft, not sure how he would react.

He put the feed bucket on the ground and stepped closer to her. "It's nothing. Just my old man being my old man." His voice was filled with bravado, but she knew there was pain underneath.

"I just didn't want to see you get hurt."

Craig took a while to answer and when he did there was more vulnerability in his voice than she'd ever heard bcfore. "I'm sorry about that first night. We were only trying to scare you. I knocked you over by accident. And I'm sorry about the way I acted. I didn't like you at first, but..." The boy's voice faltered. "You protected me from my dad today." His chin quivered. "You've been nice to me."

Morgan skirted around the horse and touched Craig's shoulder to offer support. "Thank you, Craig."

"I'm sorry for what I did, Miss Smith. I'm sorry I was mean to you." Her throat went tight as she wrapped her arms around him and gave him a hug.

Craig pulled away from Morgan and swiped at his eyes. He lifted his chin and set his jaw. His defensive shields were back up again, but it didn't matter. She'd seen the vulnerable child underneath the protective layers that helped him cope. She had a feeling this would be an end to the hostility. She continued to hold him in a sideways hug as they made their way back to camp.

Craig joined the others around the campfire.

Leaving the light provided by the camp, she walked over to a horse grazing on a patch of grass. She grabbed his reins and led him back to camp. When she looked up, Alex was headed in her direction, a sense of purpose in his step.

THIRTEEN

Alex walked toward the perimeter of the camp where Morgan was. They could not go on like this; everything seemed to cause conflict. He wasn't sure how to resolve the tension between them. He only knew he had to try.

Moonlight illuminated part of her face as she turned toward him.

He stepped closer to where she stood running her hands along a horse's back. Her long hair cascaded around her face.

"Craig has really had a turnaround. I don't think we'll have any more trouble with him," she said.

"That's good to hear." Regret ate at his insides. "I'm sorry for that crack I made about kindness not working this morning."

"But in my case, it didn't. Is that what you were thinking?" A tinge of bitterness came into her voice.

He stopped and turned to face her, bracing himself for what he had to say. "I'll be straight with you. I think you're hiding something from me. The one thing I can't deal with is deception." He shifted his weight and stared off into the distance. "My wife cheated on me with my best friend. I had my suspicions, but when she said nothing was going on, I believed her."

"Oh, Alex, I had no idea." She reached out and cupped his arm just above the elbow.

Her touch made his knees wobbly. He pulled away. "So are you going to tell me why you've closed off a whole part of yourself?"

She tilted her head sideways. Her response was slow in coming. "I…I can't." He heard the anguish in her voice.

He started walking, and she followed alongside him. Both of them knew they had more to work out.

Old suspicions rose to the surface. He'd been straight with her. It hadn't been easy to share why trust was such a huge issue with him. And she'd given him nothing in return. Maybe she was hiding from the law and that's why she'd never open up to him. He hated himself for thinking it, but he was running out of plausible explanations and excuses. "Can you tell me one thing?"

"I'll try." The soft ringing tones of her voice were like music to him.

"Are you in some sort of criminal trouble?"

She shook her head. "No," she said.

In his gut, he knew she was telling him the truth.

They walked for a while longer without saying anything. She crossed her arms over her body. "I should've grabbed a jacket."

"Here, take mine." He slipped out of his jean jacket and put it on her shoulders.

"Thank you." She stopped walking and turned to face him. "I'm so grateful for all your kindness. Please don't think I'm not."

Without thinking, his hand went up to her cheek. She was afraid of something, and she wouldn't or couldn't tell him why. He pulled his hand away. "Sorry, I shouldn't have done that."

She grabbed his hand, the warmth of her touch sinking through his skin. "There can't be anything between us." She held on to his hand, squeezing it tight.

"We have to at least find a way to work together. Can we be friends?" He wanted so much more, but he'd take what he could get.

She tilted her head, eyes searching. He could feel the force of her gaze. He leaned in closer but caught himself. His hand fluttered over her face. She'd just said there couldn't be anything between them. He needed to listen with his head and not his heart.

She put her hand over his where it rested on her cheek. "You know what I wish?"

"What?"

"I wish I'd met you at a different time and place." Her voice filled with pain.

He shook his head, not understanding. "What would it matter?"

"I think your ex-wife was a fool to let you go. You're a good man, Alex." She pulled her hand away. "I want you to know that." She turned and walked back to the camp.

Alex shook his head as confusion filled his mind. She'd said there couldn't be anything between them and yet her body language told him the exact opposite. He had heard pain in her voice, not defensiveness. If he could unlock who she was and what she was running from, maybe things could be different.

Morgan stirred from a restless sleep in her tent. Her talk with Alex had her completely bent out of shape. She loved the stables, she loved working with the horses and the children, but there was no way she could keep from hurting Alex. He was relentless in his kindness and care for her and that only made it worse. Why couldn't she have some crabby old curmudgeon for a boss?

She stared at the ceiling of her tent. Alex was the kind of man she would love for her father to meet. They would get along so well. Truth be told, if the circumstances were different, he was the kind of man she'd marry. The timing of meeting Alex was so wrong. None of this made sense. A warm tear drifted down her cheek.

She rolled over on her side and drifted off to sleep still in turmoil. She awoke to the sound of footsteps outside her tent. Someone could be getting up to go to the bathroom, but something about the way the footsteps had circled her tent put her on edge.

Her heartbeat sped up and she lay listening, tuned in to every little sound, the wind rushing through the brush and the horses whinnying in the distance. More footsteps, this time fainter and farther away, reached her ears. She pulled the sleeping bag tighter around her. As the camp fell silent again, she slowly relaxed and felt the heaviness of sleep return. Her last thoughts as she drifted off were of Alex and the risk connected with caring about him.

FOURTEEN

Morgan stared out the window of her cottage as Alex helped an owner load his horse into a trailer. They'd only been home from the trail ride a couple of days and several of the boarders had pulled out. Business must be down because of the competition.

She watched Alex make his way across the grounds, a look of raw determination on his face. She couldn't help but think that the slump in his shoulders was because of the downturn in the business.

She stared down at the phone she held in her hand. Her telling him she was leaving wouldn't make him any happier, but in the long run, it would keep his life and his heart safe. She dialed the Des Moines marshals' office.

Brendan O'Toole's voice came across the line. "Hi, Morgan. Is everything all right there?"

"Well, I'm not sure. I think someone was

creeping around my tent when I was on the trail ride." Morgan swallowed the lump in her throat. "Also, the situation here with Alex, my boss, has become complicated."

"You haven't said anything about being in witness protection, have you?"

"No, I just think it would be better if I got out of here. You said not to form attachments." She turned again to look out the window. Alex was leading a horse toward the stable. "And I've..." And she had what? Fallen in love in Alex?

"We have that rule for a good reason. When you care about someone, you start to trust them."

She found herself backpedaling, wondering if she had made the right choice. "Alex is trustworthy."

"I'm sure he is, but all he has to do is say something about you to the wrong person. I've seen it happen before," Brendan said. "Trust me, these people may not have found you yet, but they are looking. And we can't dismiss what happened to you on the trail ride. I think relocation would be prudent."

She pressed the phone harder against her ear. "I guess you're right." Her throat tightened even more as she remembered Serena's warning. Caring about people meant they were in the line of fire.

"If this was an emergency situation, we'd take you in right away to a safe house. But because it isn't, it will take us a week or so to set up the new identity and find a location for you."

"I understand." Her heart squeezed tight. This was not going to be easy. "I need time to say goodbye anyway."

"I'll be in touch with you as soon as we can set things up. I'll let the St. Louis office know what's going on, but I'll be the one to do the transport."

She hung up the phone. She pressed her hand against the glass of the window and closed her eyes.

God, please don't let Alex be too hurt by this.

It was the first prayer she had uttered since leaving Mexico. It didn't make sense that she would find a place where she was happy and loved her work only to have it taken from her again. She'd grown attached to the children and Craig. But it was Alex that she truly would miss.

She opened her eyes at a gentle knock on her door. She strode across the floor and opened the door. Alex stood on her porch.

"Stephanie Bliss, Bluebell's owner, has shown up unexpectedly." Alex's words were wrought with tension.

"Oh, yes, I remember her." He could handle getting one person out on the trail, so she had a feeling he'd knocked on her door for moral support. "Why don't I give you a hand?" The look of helplessness in Alex's eyes told her this was not the time to tell him she was leaving.

She kept up with Alex as they strode across the grounds toward the stable. Morgan could hear Bluebell banging against her stall even before she saw her.

Stephanie stood with her hands on her hips. "Good. You're here. I purchased this new saddle and I wanted to try it out." She pointed toward the English-style saddle resting on a hay bale.

Oh, great. Stephanie wanted to play dress-up with Bluebell. Morgan stepped into the horse's stall and stood off to one side. Gradually, Bluebell's antics slowed. She stopped tossing her head and stomping the ground. Bluebell snorted and then nudged Morgan with her snout.

"My, you've got the touch with her," said Stephanie. "Alex, help me get this saddle on her."

Morgan ran her hand along the animal's neck. She combed through the mane. "Can we give her a second longer? She was pretty stirred up."

Stephanie let out a huff of air and rolled her eyes. "I drove all the way out here on a weekday. I want to get the ride in as quickly as possible."

Morgan stared into the horse's dark eyes. Then she looked directly at Stephanie. "If you want to have a pleasant ride, you'll need to wait."

Stephanie's mouth dropped open. "You can't talk to me like that." She pivoted. "Alex, she can't talk to me like this."

Alex rested his hand on the stall railing. "Whatever Morgan says about the horse goes."

Stephanie's mouth dropped open. "Well, I…"

Morgan nodded toward Alex, admiration and gratitude filling her heart for him coming to her defense. Morgan leaned close to Bluebell, resting her face against the horse's warm neck.

"It's almost as if the horse likes you more than she likes me." Stephanie pouted.

"Bluebell is a good horse. All you need to do is spend time with her. I'd be glad to go with you on a trail ride. I could show you some techniques for calming her."

"You should give it a shot," Alex nudged.

Stephanie tugged at her collar and nodded in agreement. "I suppose it's worth a try."

Morgan saddled up George and met Stephanie outside. After a few hours on the trail, she started to see a change in both horse and rider. They headed back toward the stables. After getting George and Bluebell settled in their stalls, she said goodbye to Stephanie and headed across the grounds. Alex came out of the storage shed holding a clipboard. Sadness welled up inside her.

Alex tilted his head. "Everything okay?"

Every time she looked into his brown eyes, she remembered the kiss. "Yes, it's fine." Her words fell flat. She had to tell him sooner or later.

"Good. Thanks for the help with Stephanie."

"No problem. It seems quiet around here lately," she said.

He kicked the ground with his boot. "Business has dropped off a little."

She couldn't kick a man when he was down. The timing was not right yet to tell him she was leaving.

He turned to go, his boots pounding on the

hard-packed ground. He pivoted and gazed at her. "One of our clients gave me tickets to tonight's Iowa Cubs game. I don't suppose you'd want to go."

She stepped toward him. His eyes filled with vulnerability. How many times had she hurt him without intending to? "That sounds like fun. We would be going as…friends." She didn't want to mislead him any more than she had to. This would be the last time they were together, and she wanted to cherish every moment.

He nodded. "Yes, as friends." He walked backward so he was still looking at her. "Great. We'll head out in a couple hours."

She smiled. "Looking forward to it."

They drove into Des Moines underneath a cloudless sky. Alex could feel the building excitement of the crowd as they entered Principal Park and made their way toward their seats.

Morgan agreeing to go with him had fanned the embers of hope that maybe there could still be something between them. Sometimes friendship could become something more. He held her hand as they squeezed past people to settle into their seats.

The softness of Morgan's hand in his and

the sun warming his skin lifted his spirits. He felt lighter and more positive than he had felt in days. His worries over losing clients at The Stables lightened when he was with Morgan.

When they sat down, she leaned close to him, their shoulders touching. "My dad used to take me to games here when I was a kid," he told her. He went on to describe some of the more memorable moments in the games from his boyhood.

She nodded, listening. Her expression was bright and her posture relaxed, but she seemed distracted.

"Are you hungry? I can get us something to eat before the game starts."

She nodded. "A hot dog sounds great."

Alex eased past the other spectators to the aisle. As he took the stairs that led to the concession area, he noticed a man four rows back from where Morgan sat. He was a broad-shouldered man in a beige baseball cap. Judging from where the man aimed his binoculars, he seemed more interested in the spectators than the game.

Alex shook his head. Some people.

Morgan watched Alex disappear into the tunnel that led to the concession area. She stared around at the other spectators. Her attention was drawn to a man in the stands above her. He had aimed his binoculars right at her. The man wore a beige baseball cap. She turned back toward the field, feeling suddenly uncomfortable and wishing Alex was beside her. Lots of people had beige baseball caps shc rationalized.

The team mascot, a man in a bear suit wearing the blue Cubs jersey, ran out onto the field as thc announcer started with his pregame chatter. Plenty of fans were still milling through thc stands. She craned her neck to see if the man with the binoculars was still watching her. A spectator pushed past where the man was sitting. When the spectator sctled into his seat, she had a clear view of the man as he pulled his binoculars away from his face.

Her heart skipped a beat. He looked like the man who had followed her at the horse sale. She hadn't been able to ID him, but she knew him whcn she saw him.

Her mind raced as she tried to remain calm. If it was him, he wouldn't try anything in a crowd in broad daylight, would he? She gripped the arm of the seat a little tighter. When she looked again, the man had risen to his feet and was making his way through the same exit where Alex had gone.

Now she was concerned for Alex. She made her way up the stands toward where the man had exited. She followed him, checking the little pocket on the outside of her purse for her cell phone. She needed to call Brendan and get this guy picked up. Her phone was gone. Her hands trembled with fear. When they had gone through the ticket area, the crowd had been compressed into a small space. Her phone could have fallen out or someone could have lifted it.

She scanned the area, hoping to see Alex. Quite a few people were around.

She tried to keep the man in the baseball cap in sight and still maintain a safe distance. All her hopes that she hadn't been found were shattered. If her phone had been stolen, some planning had gone into this. She tried to recall the faces of the people who squeezed in around her as they entered the gate. Not the man in the baseball cap. She would have recognized him. That meant there was at least one other person in this stadium who was after her. She struggled to ignore the rising panic that made her knees feel like jelly.

She wasn't sure how it had happened or how many of the accidents were not accidents at all. Clearly, they had been watching her since the horse sale and looking for an opportunity to kill her and make it look like an accident.

They must have been watching The Stables and followed them.

She navigated through the concourse, trying to stay with the crowd. She stared at the sea of faces around her. One of these people could be working with the man in the baseball hat.

Alex made his way to his seat carrying a paper tray with two hot dogs and drinks. Morgan's seat was empty. Maybe she'd gone to the bathroom or something. He glanced around. He could sit and wait for her.

"She went up," said the man in the seat next to him.

"Up?"

The man turned and pointed. "Yeah, like she saw somebody in the stands she knew."

"Really. Thanks." Niggling suspicions danced at the corners of his mind. He scanned the seats above him and then moved to sit down. If that was the case, she'd come back when she was done visiting.

The man in the seat next to him leaned closer. "Maybe it's none of my business, but she had kind of a scared look on her face."

"She was afraid?" Still holding the food,

Alex stood back up. Maybe waiting for her to return wasn't such a good idea. Alex could hear the National Anthem being sung behind him as he took the stairs two at a time. He scanned the rows and spotted the only empty seat.

Alex bent toward the man next to the empty seat in order to be heard above the roar of the crowd. "Did a dark-haired woman go by here?"

The man cupped his ear.

Alex leaned closer and repeated his question even louder. The man stood up halfway and pointed toward an exit.

Once through the tunnel, Alex stepped out on the main concourse where the food vendors were. When he entered the concession area, the crowds had thinned substantially. He searched but found no sign of Morgan.

He stepped into a quiet area away from the noise, rested the food on a ledge and pulled out his cell phone to call her. As he listened to the phone ring three times, a hand grabbed him from behind. He'd been too focused on the phone call to register the hurried footsteps behind him.

FIFTEEN

Morgan scanned the concourse where the vendors were, hoping to see one of the security people she'd noticed earlier or a pay phone. The man in the baseball hat had disappeared, but there was still a chance he was in the stadium. The noise of the game, crowd and announcer floated in. A player had scored a home run.

With the game under way, most people were in their seats. A crowd of teenagers dispersed and she saw Beige Cap. His murderous eyes bored into her. Her heart pounded out a raging rhythm as he stepped in her direction. She turned the other way, increasing her pace. She needed to stay in this area, with customers and merchants, and not let herself get isolated. She looked over her shoulder; he was within twenty feet.

She slammed into a wall of muscle and the stench of cigars surrounded her. Cold metal pressed into her stomach. She looked up into Josef Flores's cold dark eyes.

Her breath stopped in her throat. When she looked back at Beige Cap, he offered them a salute and disappeared into a tunnel.

"Now, my dear, it seems we have some unfinished business." Josef's voice was as cold as ice.

Morgan felt as though she was shaking from the inside. The memory of Josef's attempts on her life in Mexico only intensified her fear. "You wouldn't. All these people."

He poked the gun harder against her stomach. He stood so close to her that no one could see the gun. He chuckled. "People have accidents in crowds all the time." He poked her again. "Now if you would please make your way up to the deck." He tilted his head, indicating the tunnel she needed to take.

Morgan's voice trembled when she spoke. "So you have been trying to kill me and make it look like an accident."

"I have to hand it to you. After all the failures—fire, snake, car accident—we were hopeful that something truly tragic would happen to you on that trail ride, but my man couldn't get close enough without witnesses." Josef squeezed Morgan's upper arm while still pressing the gun barrel into her back with the other hand.

There had been someone in the camp that night.

He said, "I have to tell you, between your cowboy boss and Marshal Trier, we had a hard time getting to you at all."

Fear surrounded her. Josef wouldn't be telling her this unless he intended to kill her soon. "We thought we could bide our time and wait for the right opportunity. As long as it looked like an accident there was not a huge hurry, but now it turns out you're going to leave again."

How could they have found that out? She had only told Brendan of her decision this morning.

As Josef prodded her to go up the stairs that led to the viewing platform, she glanced side to side. There had to be some way to escape.

"And if you're thinking of calling out for help, we have your friend," Josef said. "All it would take is a phone call from me, and he'd be gone. He's so protective of you. We had to make sure he was out of the way."

All the air left her lungs. She struggled to not shut down, to remain alert. She could hear the thundering footsteps and enthusiastic cheering of the crowd on the deck.

She stopped for a moment, looking up.

"A crowded balcony. Tons of drunken fans in a confined space." Josef drew out his words as though each one held a punch. "People fall all the time. Total accident."

He pushed her up the remaining steps. They merged with the crowd of fans. Squeezed in on every side, people jostled her around. The balcony was maybe ten feet wide. One side looked out on the game and the other on the parking lot below, which had to be a seventy-foot drop onto concrete, a fall no one could survive.

Morgan couldn't stop shaking as she struggled to take a deep breath. A loud cheer rose from the crowd. Most everyone was focused on the game. She leaned over to look at the field and the seats below. She could see the section where she and Alex had sat, their two empty chairs. Josef wasn't lying about Alex. She refused to give in to despair. There had to be a way out.

Josef pushed her toward the other side of the railing. She peered over the edge at the hard concrete below. The fans' focus on the game dissipated; nothing exciting was happening on the field. More people drifted closer to her as they sought out more personal space and leaned against the railing.

Josef's grip on her upper arm cut through to the nerves. He was waiting for another big play on the field, and then he would throw her over. Even though she was surrounded by people, no one would witness the fall because they would be watching the game.

Then he would just slip into the crowd while everyone stood aghast at the woman who had fallen to her death. The announcer said the next player was up to bat. Her heart seized. The crowd roared and applauded. The first pitch was a strike. The crowd grew louder and more hostile. The second pitch connected with the bat as the fans scrunched close to the opposite railing. Everyone's eyes were on the game as the player ran the bases.

Josef backed her up to the railing and prepared to land a blow to her shoulder. She tried to angle away from him, hoping someone would see what was going on. All she saw was the backs of people's heads; no one was even looking this way.

If she struggled too much, or screamed, he might shoot her and then push her over. And then what would happen to Alex? He would die, too. All because of her.

"Hey, aren't you Maryanne from Peoria?" A very drunk man squeezed in between Josef and Morgan. The man put his face close to hers. His words came out beer scented. "Don't you remember?" He placed a hand on his chest. "Richard, high-school marching band, trombone."

She peered over Richard's shoulder. Josef had been pushed several people away from her. The big play was over and the game had become uneventful again. "I think you must be mistaken." She took advantage of the separation and pushed through the crowd as fast as she could.

She squeezed between two large men. At one point, she felt a tug on her shirt hem, but she persevered, pushing through the crowd. Even though he had a gun, Josef wouldn't try anything that would peg him as guilty. Finally, she arrived at the stairwell and hurried down. He couldn't be far behind her. Once she was downstairs, she slipped behind a janitorial cleaning cart. The minutes ticked by and she waited for her heart rate to return to normal.

When she peered above the cart, she thought she saw a man who looked like Josef go by. A realization sank in that sent shivers over her skin. Josef had revealed himself to her and all but confessed. His determination to make sure she didn't get out of the stadium alive now would be stronger than ever.

She moved out from behind the cart. As afraid as she was, she had to find Alex and help him.

She knew the clock was ticking. Alex didn't deserve to die, especially not because of her.

She ran out onto the main concourse toward the concession area; wave after wave of panic forced her feet to move faster. She ran toward the T-shirt vendor, who had no customers. She still had options, and she wasn't going down without a fight.

Glancing side to side, she nearly slammed against the counter. "Please, can I borrow your phone?"

A stunned look crossed the clerk's face. "Are you okay?"

"It's an emergency. I need to borrow your phone." Her voice was jittery, filled with fear.

"Do you want me to get security?"

Morgan thought for a moment. "Tell them that there are two men in this stadium who have committed a crime."

The girl pulled her cell phone from her purse and pressed in a phone number. She glanced nervously at Morgan several times. Someone came on the line. "Hey Max, there's a woman here who says she spotted two men who have committed a crime." She listened for a moment, nodded and then hung up. She looked at Morgan. "He'll come and talk to you."

"No, that's not going to work. We don't have that kind of time. They can't let these guys leave the stands." She thought for a moment. "Please let me have your phone."

If she couldn't make sure Josef and his thug were caught, she needed to get out of here. The woman's hand moved in slow motion. Morgan took the phone and stepped away from the vendor booth. She couldn't have the clerk overhearing the conversation.

"Hey, where are you taking my phone?" The girl skirted around the counter and grabbed the phone back.

"I wasn't going to steal it. I just need to make a private call."

The suspicious look on the clerk's face remained, but she backed away. Morgan dialed the number of her contact in Des Moines. Brendan picked up on the first ring.

"I'm in a life-threatening situation. I've been found. I need to be brought in."

"Where are you?"

"Principal Park," she said.

"I can be there in twenty minutes. I'll be in a blue SUV." Brendan sounded as though he was walking as he spoke on the phone. A sense of urgency colored his words.

"I'll look for you, but I can't be out in the open." She glanced side to side, aware that she couldn't stay out here much longer, either. "I need to get out of this stadium."

"There's an employee parking lot to the east of the entrance. There will be people there, and it won't be the first place these guys would look for you."

Her heart raced at the prospect of having to wait while Josef and the other man were still looking for her. "Got it."

Morgan slapped the phone down on the counter.

"Aren't you going to stay put until security gets here?" The clerk held the phone protectively to her chest.

She couldn't wait around like a sitting duck. She needed to keep moving. "One of the men has a white suit and is Mexican, and the other has a round face and wears a beige baseball cap." She doubted they would be caught, but she had to try.

She took several steps back. She needed to get out of here, but first, as afraid as she was of Josef catching her, she had to find Alex. Once Brendan picked her up, she'd never see him again. She needed to leave knowing he was safe.

Her worry over what might have happened

to Alex increased. It could be that he had only gone looking for her, but the threats Josef had made pierced through her all over again. She walked faster.

A roar came up from the stadium and then quieted. A dozen or so spectators trailed into the concession area. Morgan fought off the panic that invaded her muscles and fogged her thinking. The last time she'd seen Alex he was going to get hot dogs for them. She ran over to the hot dog vendor.

The clerk was a college-age girl. "What can I get for you?"

She glanced around, fearing that Josef or Beige Cap would appear. "There was a man here maybe a half an hour ago. Western-cut blue shirt. Dark curly hair."

"I remember him. Good-looking guy. The reason why I remember him is I saw him walk by about five minutes after he bought his food, still holding it. Weird."

"Which way did he go?"

She pointed toward the far end of the concourse. "By the janitor's closet."

Morgan hurried in that direction. Beige Cap came around the corner. Heart racing, she slipped into an alcove and waited as he stalked past her, his face distorted with rage.

She found the janitor's closet. Two hot

dogs and drinks were strewn across the concrete. She tried the doorknob. It was locked. She banged on the door. "Alex." Her voice cracked, giving away the level of urgency she felt. "Alex, are you in there?"

She didn't hear anything. She banged again.

Oh God, let me be in time.

"What are you doing? That area is for employees only." A man pushing a garbage can on wheels glared at her.

"Please, you have to let me in here. There's a man in there. He's in danger." The man's tight expression suggested that he didn't believe her. "Please, you must have a key. Open it for me. What can it hurt?"

His look softened, and he took a step toward her. "I've seen some crazy things in my life." He pulled out his keys and shoved one in the lock.

Morgan dashed into the long narrow room. Alex wasn't here. She stared at the wall of cleaning supplies. What had happened to him? Had Josef lied so she wouldn't raise a ruckus when he dragged her up to the deck?

The janitor stood behind her. "Ma'am?"

Her mind raced as her stomach clenched. Realization rose to the surface of her awareness. Josef would not have come out in the open like that unless he intended to kill her. She was cut off from the people who could help her. She wasn't going to get out of this stadium alive. "I'm sorry. I've made a mistake." She hurried back out toward the main concourse.

She glanced around at the fans and the vendors. What could she do? If Josef had been lying to keep her in the stadium, was it possible Alex was okay? She ran toward the tunnel that led to where they'd been sitting. She had to know that he was safe.

A voice sounded behind her. "Morgan."

She turned. Alex ran toward her. Overjoyed, she fell into his arms. "I was so afraid." She looked into his face. He had a cut above his eyebrow.

"Some guy tried to push me into a janitor's closet. He didn't see my left hook coming, but then he ran away. I need to go down to the police station and file a report."

She touched his face, unable to contain the elation she felt at his being unharmed. "I'm so glad you're okay." Her joy turned to terror. Next time, Alex might not get away. "You make sure you go to the police, Alex. Give them the description of the man who did this to you." She turned and started walking.

He grabbed her arm. "Where are you going?"

She pulled away from him. She might die here today but she wasn't taking Alex down with her. Josef's threat was very real. "I have to go. Stay away from me."

He pointed to the cut on his forehead. "This is connected to you, isn't it? Who was that guy?"

"Please just stay away from me," she pleaded. She ran toward the entrance. When she looked over her shoulder, Alex had been slowed down by a crowd of people. She exited the stadium and stared at the streets around her and people passing by. No sign of Josef, but that didn't mean she was in the clear.

She started walking, scanning the parking lot for her contact's car or the police. Twenty minutes hadn't passed since she'd made the call. She moved from one cluster of people to another while she watched the street.

Within minutes the blue SUV pulled up to the curb, and Brendan got out. His gaze darted from side to side. Morgan breathed a sigh of relief and made her way toward him across the concrete expanse. She walked fast, trying not to draw attention to herself.

Recognition spread across his face when he saw her. In a little while, this would all be over. They'd take her to a safe house. She'd start a new life somewhere…without Alex.

Brendan stepped toward her. Then she heard a high-pitched popping sound and Brendan crumpled to the ground.

SIXTEEN

Morgan felt as though she'd hit an invisible wall. Brendan lay on the ground, not moving. She looked up and all around the lot, not sure where the shot had come from. She could not even process what had just happened. Her first impulse was to run to see if Brendan was still alive.

Before she took a step, Morgan felt a man's arm wrap around her neck. He yanked her back.

"Stay away from her." Alex's voice was strong and steady. He landed a blow to the man's jaw that knocked him flat. This was not Beige Cap. It was a different man. His suit jacket flopped open and she saw the gun.

A car screeched into the lot. Josef was behind the wheel.

Alex grabbed her hand. "Come on, let's go."

She glanced over her shoulder as the man

got to his feet. Two people had rushed over to where Brendan lay. Alex dragged her past the stadium toward the spectator parking lot as the thug pushed himself to his feet and chased after them. They ducked behind the cars, weaving their way toward Alex's car.

He jerked the car door open. He looked at her, fire in his eyes. "We need to go down to the police station."

She looked over her shoulder. The thug's head bobbed above the cars about five rows away. Their pursuer was closing in. The only other people in the huge parking lot were far away.

"No, please!" She pushed Alex away.

"I'm not leaving you here with that guy coming after you. What kind of man do you think I am?"

She could feel her determination shrinking. She was tired, tired of running, tired of looking over her shoulder. Tired of living in a constant state of fear. What did it matter if they got her? But they could not hurt Alex. "Please, I'm poison to you. Just stay away from me."

The man was within a hundred yards, and he was headed straight for them. The thug reached his hand into his belt to get his gun. Alex yanked open the driver's door and pushed her in as a shot was fired. She screamed and ducked down. Through the windshield she could see the man running toward them.

Alex pressed on the gas and backed out, spraying pebbles as he zoomed toward the street. She looked out the back window. Her pursuer had stopped running and was talking on his cell phone, probably getting Josef to pick him up.

Alex zigzagged through traffic. An ambulance sped past them headed to the stadium, probably to give aide to Brendan. She was grateful someone had been there to help him.

She gripped the armrest. "Where are you going?"

"To the police." He set his jaw. "I'll take you there." She saw then that he wasn't going to give up. His sense of duty meant he wouldn't let her go if he thought she was in danger. His goodness might get him killed. She had to get away from him as quickly as possible. But just walking away wouldn't work, not with Alex.

She closed her eyes. At this point, going to the police seemed the only viable solution. Brendan was severely wounded or dead. She could call the marshals in St. Louis from there. Alex would be safe in the police station. She could walk out of there and out of his life.

Her heart squeezed tight. "You didn't ask me who those people were."

He stared at the road ahead as traffic grew even heavier. "I knew you wouldn't tell me," he said.

"The less you know, the better." She craned her neck. Josef's car had slipped in behind them. "We have to lose these guys first. There are people who can help me. But we have to get away from these men."

Alex gripped the steering wheel and checked the rearview mirror. These guys acted like hired killers. Just what had Morgan gotten herself involved with? There would be a time for explaining but for now they needed to get to a safe place.

He came within blocks of the police station but the car was right behind them. He'd seen what they were capable of. They'd shot one man in broad daylight. They probably wouldn't have any qualms about shooting them on the police station steps.

Alex turned suddenly onto a side street. His turn was so abrupt that Morgan slammed against her window. "Sorry about that. We can't seem to shake our tail."

Morgan gripped the dashboard. “Maybe if we went out on the highway and got up some speed. We could double back to the police station.”

“I don’t know if that will work.” He zoomed up a wide boulevard where the speed limit was higher than city streets. He checked the rearview mirror. The dark car was still behind them. “Why don’t you tell me what would work? Do you know what is going on?”

She stared out the window. “There are people who can help me,” she said again. “I would need to make a call.”

He came to a freeway entrance and took the exit. Their pursuers followed. He touched his shirt pocket where he kept his phone. It was empty. He must have dropped it during the assault at the stadium.

Morgan’s face registered disappointment. “We have to get to a phone.”

“We can go back to The Stables,” he said. He increased his speed and passed several cars.

Morgan craned her neck to look at the cars behind her. “They’d be expecting that.”

Why were these guys after her? He watched the signs on the highway. “I have a friend who owns a hobby farm not too far from here. It’s down a bunch of unmarked country roads.

We might be able to throw these guys off that way. We can call from my friend's house."

"It's worth a shot, but we have to make sure they haven't followed us."

Alex drove on the highway for another twenty minutes before turning off into a wooded area. They passed plowed fields and several barns and farmhouses.

Morgan stared out the window not saying anything. The only thing that gave away the level of tension she felt was her tightly laced fingers resting on her lap.

He had a dozen theories why these men were after her. She'd assured him that she wasn't involved in criminal activity. After what he had seen today, doubts had begun to creep in. He wanted to believe her, but he also didn't want to be anyone's chump ever again.

She looked over at him. "You didn't have to do this. To help me."

"I did have to. I saw what those guys were capable of." He turned onto a long straight road. There wasn't so much as a dust cloud behind them.

"After we get to your friend's house and my help comes, you're off the hook."

He shook his head. "Is that what you think I want, to be off the hook?"

"It's the way it has to be." Her voice was tainted with hurt or maybe it was regret.

His friend's farm came into view. Still no sign of the pursuer's car. "Tell me one thing. Do you care for me at all?"

She remained silent for a long time. "A great deal, Alex."

And yet she couldn't get away from him fast enough. She didn't want his help. He didn't understand it. He parked the car in front of a single-level home and turned to face her. "I would have wanted to be with you even if you could never tell me about your past. I just wanted to be with you."

Her eyes glazed. She turned away. "Let's go make that phone call." Her voice had become robotic, as if she was trying to hide her emotions. She was pushing him away with her words.

He opened the car door. He walked up to the house and knocked on the door. Morgan came up behind him. He knocked a second time. Morgan peered through a window. "I don't see anyone inside."

He tried the door, which was locked. "His truck is here. He might be in the barn or out in the field on his tractor."

They walked across the grounds toward a barn that was at least a hundred yards from the house. When he looked over at her, her long dark hair had worked loose of the braid. He froze a picture of her in his mind, the soft angles of her face and that contemplative look she had. He knew in that moment that he loved her, but he could not make her stay no matter what he said. She simply would not or could not let him in.

He opened the barn door and hollered for his friend. "Clarence." The barn contained mostly farm equipment, a motorcycle and a pen with several sheep in it. Dust twirled around in the light that streamed in from the roof.

Morgan came up behind him. "How far away from the house is this field that he might be in?"

"Can't see it from here." He moved toward the front of the barn.

"I don't think it's a good idea to stay put." Fear permeated her voice.

He rubbed his eyes. "Let's check around the property a little more." He walked around to the far side of the barn and stared out into the field. He didn't even see a dust cloud that might be a tractor stirring up things.

When they came around the other side of the barn, the pursuer's dark-colored truck was parked by theirs. Alex drew a protective arm toward Morgan as a gasp escaped her mouth.

A rifle shot zinged through the air. He pulled Morgan to the ground and threw his body over her. There was no time to process what was happening. A second shot broke through the silence. Where were the shots coming from?

He rolled away from her, scanning the area. The shooter was perched in the bed of the truck, resting his rifle on the cab. "Seek cover." He grabbed her hand and pulled her toward a pile of unstacked firewood.

They half ran, half crawled toward the firewood, then dove behind it.

"We can't get back to the car." Her voice faltered. "What do we do?"

He stared at her, fear etched across her face. "I'll get you out of this."

She shook her head. "I'm so sorry. I never meant for you to get involved."

He angled his head around the wood. Another shot hit a log above him, inches from his head. He grabbed her hand and pulled her toward the field. "This way."

Morgan kept up with him as they ran for tree cover. He willed his legs to pump harder.

He didn't know the area around his friend's house that well, but they had passed farmhouses on the twisted road in. He glanced over his shoulder. The assailant's truck crossed the grounds, coming straight toward them.

As the truck charged toward them, he wondered if they would make it to one of those farmhouses.

Morgan ran hard to keep up with Alex. The overturned field they ran through was muddy from the excessive rain, which slowed the truck down. She said a prayer of thanks for that. They ran toward a fledgling forest. The truck would have to go around the trees, which bought them a little more time.

They ran until the trees thinned and the land around them was flat. There was nothing to use for cover. That made them sitting ducks. In the distance, the sun glinted off the metal of the truck.

Alex stopped and waited for her to catch up with him. "We need to get to a trail where he can't follow in that truck."

By now the marshals must have been informed that Brendan had been shot. They'd come looking for her, but they wouldn't know where to look. Would they mount an all-out search for her or be more covert?

Alex veered toward a part of the landscape

with more growth. He grabbed her hand and pulled her behind a bush that was just beginning to leaf out. She heard the rumble of the truck before she saw it. She peered out between the branches as the truck slowed to a crawl.

Her heart pounded so violently she thought it would break her rib cage. The truck drove off away from them, then stopped. The shooter jumped out of the bed of the truck and walked straight toward them.

She tugged on Alex's sleeve. "We have to go."

Alex pointed at the bare landscape around them. "No cover," he whispered.

The shooter drew closer, still walking directly toward them. Did he see them? She crouched lower, grateful that both of them were wearing colors that blended with the surroundings. The shooter's gaze darted around as he turned side to side. He hadn't spotted them yet.

Then Josef got out of the truck.

The shooter drew within twenty feet of them. He was the same man who had chased them outside at the stadium. Morgan held her breath. The raging beat of her heart surrounded her. Alex pressed close to her. His shoulder warmed hers. Even though she knew it was wrong to have dragged Alex into this, she was grateful that he was here. She didn't have to face this danger alone.

Josef shouted something. The shooter stopped, turned and trotted back to the truck. A moment later, the truck started up and drove parallel to where they were hiding.

When the rumble of the truck faded, Alex tugged on her shirt and they ran out into the open. Both of them glanced over their shoulders from time to time. They kept running as the sky grew darker. Morgan fought not to give in to despair. They had no weapons, no phone, no car and no food. The marshals didn't know where she was and neither of them knew this area at all.

"Do you think we should try to go back to your friend's house?" she said.

"We've been running for hours," said Alex. "My guess is if they don't find us, they'll wait for us to go back that way. It's too big a risk."

As it grew dark, they came out on what looked like a country road that was no longer used. Grass and bushes sprouted out of the flat area where cars used to drive.

"Up there." Alex pointed.

She could see the silhouette of a building. They ran toward it. Even before they got close, the condition of the overgrown yard told her the house was abandoned. A door hung on its hinges. Windows were broken out.

"I'll look around the property. Maybe there's a pump or some sort of water source."

"I'll see what's inside." The wooden stairs creaked as she went up them. Before going inside, she turned and scanned the area. No sign of a truck anywhere. She stepped past the dangling door. Bile rose up in her throat at the smell. The place was probably crawling with mice. In the dust-laden cupboard, she found a chipped mug, a ceramic bowl and a sealed plastic container with a few pieces of macaroni in it. The other rooms of the house revealed grimy clothes and a mattress. A bottle of mouthwash had been left in the bathroom medicine cabinet. She also located a back entrance.

She heard footsteps in the house. Alex poked his head into the room where she was. "There's a creek not too far to the east."

She held up the cup and the bowl. "I found these. And if you like pasta, I have three pieces of macaroni that we can cook."

He laughed. "At least we have water."

She followed him outside through the dark. The creek trickled over rocks, creating a simple melody. She kneeled by the rushing water and handed him the plastic container. “This is probably the cleanest since it was sealed.”

He dumped the few pieces of macaroni on the ground. “Maybe we’ll have that pasta feast some other time.”

His joke served to lift her spirits. Why was he so willing to go through all this for her without complaint? This was not his battle. As she splashed water on her face, she thought about what he had said earlier. That he would accept her if she never told him a thing about her past. If a man was willing to accept her on those terms and he was willing to go through all that he had gone through.... Alex had shown how much he cared about her through his actions.

He washed the container, filled it and handed it to her. The cool water was like honey to her dry throat. She handed the container back to him, and he refilled it.

She held up the bottle of mouthwash. “Maybe we can rinse this out and take some water with us.”

“I think we should stay here for the night.”

Morgan tensed. “But they might find us.”

“They went in the opposite direction. If we keep going, we could end up running into them. I say we stay here for the night and get rested up. In the morning, I’ll have a clearer idea of where we're at and how we can get to a place that has a phone, so you can call for help." A silence settled between them. When he did speak, his voice had slipped into a lower register. "Who is it you are calling for help anyway?"

She knew what he was asking. He wanted the truth from her. He had risked everything and nearly lost his life for her. All without knowing who she was or why she had pushed him away. They might not live to see the morning. He deserved to hear the truth. "Why do you think those men are after me?"

"A crazy ex-boyfriend wouldn't go to all this trouble. Either you're tied up with the mafia or you're in some sort of witness protection program."

"Which one do you vote for?"

He scooted toward her. Moonlight washed over his face. "The second one."

She nodded.

"So Morgan isn't even your real name." He sounded angry. The angles of his face were taut and his mouth was a hard straight line.

Of course he was angry. She didn't blame him. She shook her head. "My name is Magdalena."

"Magdalena." He repositioned himself on

the grass. He crossed his legs and leaned back, resting his weight on his hands.

She had longed to hear him say her name, her real name. But not like this. She couldn't see his face clearly anymore, but she could feel the heaviness between them. His silence was not unexpected. He had been caring and kind and she had deceived him.

She should have left the day she felt her heart opening up to him.

He rose to his feet, turned his back to her and leaned a hand against a nearby tree. Why didn't he shout at her? The silence was harder to take than overt anger.

"Not everyone in the Witness Security Program is innocent," he said.

She understood what he was getting at. He was trying to figure out what kind of a person she really was, what part of her was real and what part was an act. "I haven't committed a crime. I wasn't lying when I said that earlier. I witnessed a crime." She could only imagine the gut-wrenching pain he was going through right now after what his ex-wife had done to him. "I'm sorry. I should have left when I—"

He whirled around. His words filled with accusation. "When you what?"

"When I started having feelings for you," she said.

He nodded but didn't say anything.

"What I did was wrong. If I had just left, you wouldn't be here in this mess." Regret ate at her gut.

He took his time in responding. "We should find a safe place to rest for the night." He walked toward the house.

She followed behind, staring at his back as her heart broke for the turmoil he must feel. He stepped into the kitchen and looked around. He then slipped to the floor, using the lower cupboards as a backrest.

She came and sat a few feet from him. Even though she was exhausted, she didn't think she would be able to sleep. His anger was palpable. She drew her knees up to her chest and stared at the ceiling.

Gradually her eyelids became heavy and her muscles relaxed. Right before she drifted off, he placed his jean jacket over her shoulders. It was still warm from his body heat. Alex couldn't help but take care of her and protect her despite the hard feelings she had created. Caring was instinctual for him. Again, sorrow surrounded her. How could such a perfect man enter her life at the perfectly wrong time?

She laid her head on the hard floor and sleep came.

SEVENTEEN

Alex slept in short fitful increments. He awoke several times, rose quietly to his feet and checked for movement or light through the broken windows. Blackness stared back at him. Wind caused metal to creak and rustled the grass.

Morgan looked peaceful as she slept, though the hard floor couldn't be that comfortable. Or should he call her Magdalena? He clenched his teeth. He'd been angry when she'd finally come clean. Her deception had been a grand one. What bothered him more than anything was that even after her revelation, his feelings for her still smoldered. But who was he even attracted to? She wasn't who she said she was. Had she been pretending about everything, or had some of the moments between them been genuine? She had said that she cared about him.

He paced through the house, treading lightly.

Still, he understood why she needed to hide who she was. If the men who had come after her were any indication, her life was under extreme threat.

He sat down in a kitchen chair that had the back broken off. Her secret was safe with him. He wouldn't have told anyone. Why didn't she trust him in the first place? The anguish he felt over Morgan was worse than dealing with the two hoodlums who were chasing them. Hopefully, he could get Morgan to a safe place and then, what, say goodbye to her? Obviously, she couldn't stay here.

She was in witness protection, which was maybe one step up from being on the run. He had a good life at The Stables, a settled life. He saw now how untenable a relationship with her would be. It didn't matter that he loved her.

The thought of life without her sent a stab of pain through his chest. She did matter to him. A big piece of his life would be missing when she was gone.

The fog of sleep invaded his troubled thoughts and he nodded off where he sat. He jerked awake, not knowing if an hour or ten minutes had passed. It was still dark outside. The hairs on the back of his neck stood up. Something in the atmosphere had shifted, even though he couldn't see or hear anything that alarmed him.

He rose to his feet. It was hard to see in the dark, but nothing looked amiss through the windows. He stepped out onto the rickety porch. The headlights seemed to come out of nowhere, suddenly appearing on the overgrown road.

Adrenaline coursed through him, and he rushed back inside to get Morgan.

"Wake up—they're here."

"What?" She still wasn't coherent.

He pulled her to her feet. "Does this place have a back door?"

Now he could hear the rumbling of the diesel engine.

Outside, truck doors slammed and voices grew louder.

"I think it's this way." Morgan ran through the dark house, bumping into a wall.

He grabbed her hand so he wouldn't lose her in the dark.

The thugs' footsteps pounded on the floorboards as one barked orders at the other.

"It's around here somewhere," she whispered. She felt along the wall and slipped into yet another room. He saw the doorway before she did. He pulled her through it.

Footsteps pounded behind them as they

headed toward an open field. He looked over his shoulder where lights shone. A rifle shot zinged through the air, missing them by quite a bit. At least the darkness provided some cover.

She stumbled and fell. "My foot's caught." Panic filled her voice.

He dropped to the ground, unable to see what she'd gotten tangled up in. It looked like wire that was anchored in place, maybe part of an old fence. His hand wrapped around her foot and he tried to pry the wire apart.

Behind them, lights bobbed across the field.

"Go without me," she said. "This is not your fight. We both don't have to die."

This *was* his fight because he cared about what happened to her. "I'm not leaving you." He spoke through clenched teeth as he pulled harder on the wires.

The sound of the two men shouting pressed on them. The pursuers spread farther apart, waving the flashlights in broad arcs. His arm muscles strained as he pulled hard on the wire that surrounded her foot.

"There, I think I can get out," she said.

One of the pursuers was thirty yards from them and closing in fast. They'd been spotted.

He helped her to her feet and they ran. The

terrain changed as they came to a grassy field with some bushes. The man behind them was close enough that they could hear his footsteps.

Morgan had slowed down. She must have hurt her ankle. He looked over his shoulder just as the thug grabbed her. She screamed as he put his hands around her neck.

Alex landed a hard left hook to the man's jaw and another to his stomach. The thug reeled backward, falling on the ground on his behind. The man groaned and then reached inside his coat, probably for his gun.

Alex felt a surge of fear-driven strength as he grabbed Morgan's hand and bolted. Darkness still provided cover. That was probably why the thug had tried to catch up with them in the first place instead of shooting in the dark with a handgun that didn't have much range. Morgan lagged behind, favoring one foot. He didn't let go of her hand. He pulled her ahead of him just as a shot was fired.

He shielded her from the thug until he was sure they had shaken him. The man was big and muscular but not much of a runner. They might be able to stay ahead of him. The other man, the one with the rifle, was younger and in better shape. Hopefully he had gone so far in the wrong direction that he wouldn't ever catch up.

They came out on a dirt road with a barbwire fence running alongside it. This road looked used, but it was unlikely anyone would be passing this way at this time of night.

Morgan stopped on the road, out of breath and panting. "Should we follow it and see if it leads us to a house?"

Alex glanced around. No sign of the bobbing flashlights anywhere. "Let's stay off on the side there by that fence. We won't be so visible."

The road stretched out before him. Did it matter which way they went? He picked a direction and started walking. Morgan followed.

Hours later, the sky turned from black to charcoal. Dawn could not be far off. He prayed they would make it to see the sunrise.

They heard a distant rumble of a vehicle. Headlights appeared around the bend.

"Get down just in case it's them." He pulled her toward the edge of the road.

She plunged down in the grass. "But what if it's someone who can help us?"

The vehicle drew closer. He lay down in the grass beside her, peering over the top of the road. "It's not a chance I'm willing to take. I'll try to figure out what it is before it passes us." The headlights were higher off the ground, like a truck's.

The chances of a vehicle that wasn't their pursuers going by here at this time of the morning was slim. The vehicle was traveling at not more than twenty miles an hour.

The seconds ticked by. The outline of the car became clearer. It looked more like an SUV than a truck. The car crept past them.

Alex jumped up to the road and waved his arms, running toward the car. It slowed and then stopped. A dark figure stepped out onto the road.

Morgan's footsteps sounded behind him.

"What on earth are you folks doing out here in the middle of the night?"

Alex held out his hand for the man to shake. "It's a long story, sir, but if you could take us somewhere where we could call…a friend. Or if you have a phone we could borrow."

"Sure, I can do that. I don't have one of those cell phones with me. I'm sure we can find an all-night diner or something in the little town up ahead."

He could see the man more clearly now, short hair, middle-aged. It wasn't anyone he knew. He turned toward Morgan. "You want to take the front seat?"

Her answer was slow in coming. “Why don’t we sit together in the back?”

“Sure.” She was still pretty shaken up from their near-death experience. Her sitting so close stirred up a mixture of negative and positive emotions. As they slipped into the backseat, he wondered why she had hesitated in answering.

Had she seen something about this guy that set off alarm bells for her?

Morgan only half listened to the conversation between Alex and their rescuer. Maybe she’d been running for too long and been caught off guard one too many times, but something about this driver felt wrong to her.

The license plates were from out of state. That in itself didn’t make the man guilty. It seemed odd, though, that someone not from here would be driving around in the predawn hours.

“So what brings you to this neck of the woods?” Alex asked. His hands slipped over hers. She didn’t blame him if he was still angry at her, but she was grateful for the calming effect of his touch.

“Up here for a funeral, sad to say. Drove all night,” said the man.

A logical explanation, but she still couldn't let go of her suspicions.

In the predawn light, plowed fields and cows came into view. She had no idea where they were. She didn't know this area at all. "Where are you taking us?"

"I'm thinking there is a little gas station up the road a piece, if memory serves. Haven't been back to these parts in some time."

"What is the gas station called?" Alex asked.

"Don't remember the name of it. Like I said, it's been a long time since I was back here."

The tone of Alex's voice had changed and his back stiffened. Was he growing suspicious, too? "Isn't this Gregson's Road?"

"I'm not familiar with the names around here. It seems that I remember a crossroads up here with a gas station." The man's voice remained steady despite the pressing questions. "That's all I know."

They drove past a cluster of trees. The man slowed and pulled over to the shoulder.

Morgan tensed and glanced in Alex's direction.

"You folks will have to excuse me for a moment. That thirty-two ounce soda I had a while back is catching up with me."

The man pushed the door open and disappeared behind some trees.

Morgan let out her breath. "I can't help myself. I'm just really paranoid about who this guy is."

"Me, too. He seems aboveboard but…" Alex shook his head. "After yesterday, it's hard to believe anyone could be a nice person." He pushed the door open and tilted his head in the direction the man had disappeared. "I'm going to stretch my legs. You might want to get out, too."

Was Alex thinking that they might need to run? Morgan scooted across the seat and stood beside Alex. "Why did you ask him if we were on Gregson's Road?"

"There is no Gregson's Road. I thought maybe I could trip him up," Alex said.

"Honestly, he hasn't done or said anything—"

He grabbed her hand, his eyes growing wide. "Listen."

The faint noise of a one-sided conversation drifted over from the trees where the man had disappeared. The man had said he didn't have a cell phone. She could hear only bits and pieces of the conversation like "deliver them" and "finish the job." And then she heard the name Josef.

Her fear revved into overdrive. "He said he didn't have a cell phone. We have to get out of here."

Alex opened the driver's door. "He took the keys." He grabbed her hand. "Let's go. Come on."

They ran up the road. The man emerged from the trees and raced toward his car. Alex veered off the road just as the man started up his car. The car gained speed. There was no cover around them, only an open field.

The car swerved off the road and charged toward them, slowed only by the plowed furrows.

"You keep going." Alex shouted as he slowed down. He kneeled to pick something off the ground as the car drew closer.

Morgan sprinted. She glanced over her shoulder as the car closed in on Alex. He lifted his hand and threw something at the windshield. The car slowed and Alex ran toward it. Though it was still moving, he yanked open the driver's door and pummeled the driver as he ran alongside the car. The car hit a stump and stopped.

Morgan ran toward the fight as Alex pulled the man out of the car and hit him hard across the jaw. The man crumpled to the ground. He was conscious but disoriented. Alex leaned down and pulled the handgun out of the man's waistband.

Alex didn't need to tell her what to do. She got into the passenger side as he stepped over the thug and slipped behind the steering wheel.

Alex turned the key in the ignition. The car churned but didn't turn over.

The thug on the ground was starting to push himself to his feet.

"Try again." This car was their only hope. No doubt, the man had phoned Josef and his friend who had chased them earlier. They would be on their way to finish them off.

Alex turned the key in the ignition. The engine started up though it still sputtered. Morgan screamed as the thug made his way to her side of the car.

Alex shifted into Reverse. Morgan hit the door lock just as the man reached for the outside handle. The thug plastered his face to the window and pounded with his fists.

"Hope this car makes it. Something might have been damaged in the crash." Alex turned the wheel and pressed the accelerator again.

The man picked up a rock and slammed it against Morgan's window. Morgan edged toward Alex, whose gaze darted everywhere as he pressed the accelerator a second time. The car made a screeching sound but didn't move.

The man continued to pound on the window, cracking it. Morgan screamed and leaned closer to Alex as broken glass flew across the seat. The man reached in to open the car door.

Alex picked up the gun where he had placed it on the dashboard and pointed it at the man.

The man stepped back, holding up his hands. "Please, Josef paid me to find you guys. I'm not a killer." He took another step back. "And this is not worth dying for."

"Just let us go then." Alex handed the gun over to Morgan. "Keep this pointed at him."

Alex tried to restart the car. This time the engine turned over. Alex circled around the man and eased the car onto the road. The engine noises indicated that the car was not running at a hundred percent. The man in the field grew smaller as Alex drove.

Morgan struggled to catch her breath. "That guy probably told Josef and his helper where we are when he made that call."

Alex stared at the road ahead. "Yeah, and he was taking us to them. We could be driving straight toward Josef."

She rested her forehead in her palm as

panic coiled around her and squeezed the breath from her lungs. "We didn't take his cell phone. He'll call Josef, tell him we got away and what direction we're headed."

Alex shook his head and pounded a fist against the steering wheel. "We could have used that cell phone, too."

He checked the rearview mirror. They both knew it was too late and too dangerous to go back for the phone.

As the car inched up the road, she stared through the windshield, wondering how long they had before Josef tracked them down.

EIGHTEEN

Alex wasn't sure what was damaged, but the SUV had a top speed of thirty. They'd passed by fields and barns and cows and still found no sign of civilization. The rising sun, still low on the horizon, warmed the car.

"There," said Morgan. She pointed across the field to a bunch of trees surrounding a house. At last. He turned off on the long straight road. A truck and car were parked outside the brick farmhouse. Light glowed in the kitchen but the other windows were dark.

A bike and two tricycles were propped against the porch and a swing set resided in the side yard.

"Small children live here." Morgan's voice was barely above a whisper and filled with anxiety.

He could guess at what she was thinking. Would the people who were after her harm a family to get to her? "These people who can help you can get here pretty fast, right?"

"I don't know. I assume they've been looking for me." She ran her fingers through her hair. "We're miles from The Stables, though."

The Stables. His job there felt like it had existed a lifetime ago. What was going to happen now? The law enforcement people would whisk Morgan away, and he would never see her again. And he would go back to what? A much emptier life.

He knocked on the door. A woman came to the door and opened it. Her blond hair was pulled up in a careless ponytail and a toddler rested on her hip. She stared at them. Her expression was neither hostile nor welcoming. She was probably wondering what two ragged-looking strangers in a beat-up car were doing in her yard so early in the morning.

"Ma'am, I'm sorry to bother you, but we…" He hesitated as his thoughts raced. What plausible explanation could he offer that wouldn't give Morgan away?

Morgan stepped forward. "Our car is on its last legs. It's not running well. If we could borrow your phone, we can call a friend to come and get us."

She'd had a little more practice in maintaining a cover story.

The woman bounced the toddler and studied them from head to toe. They must look pretty bad after their all-night run and two fights. "Most people have cell phones these days."

"Please, you can bring the phone out to the porch. We won't bother you. I understand why this must look strange." Morgan sounded as though she were near tears.

The woman's expression softened. "You can come in." She tilted her head. "My husband's just over there by the barn."

The comment was designed to let them know she hadn't totally let her suspicions go. Her husband would come to her rescue if needed. They followed the woman into the brightly lit kitchen, where she placed the toddler in a high chair. "Phone's in the living room." She spoke without drawing her attention away from the baby.

The living room was dimly lit. Only a single floor lamp was turned on. Morgan picked up the phone and wandered toward a dark corner.

After all they'd been through, she was still being secretive. She was probably right. The less Alex knew, the better. He assumed the

U.S. Marshals would let him go back to his old life. The only problem was he was having a hard time picturing himself there without Morgan.

By this afternoon, she'd be halfway across the country with a new name.

Still holding the phone, Morgan wandered into the kitchen to ask the woman her exact address.

A few minutes later, she hung up the phone and turned to face him. "They can be here in half an hour. Their GPS shows a field not too far away from here with and an old barn The barn is falling down and looks like it hasn't been used in years they said."

"At least let me go with you to make sure you're safely in custody. After that, I can probably get that car to a place where a friend can come get me."

"They'll bring the car in for evidence and fingerprints. They want you to come, too. They have to interview you and find out how much you know."

"And then..."

She shook her head. "I don't know what they'll decide."

So what did that mean? That he wouldn't be able to go back to his old life if he knew too much? Would they put him in witness protection, too?

She stepped toward him. "I'm sorry that you have to go through this. All because you tried to help me."

Perhaps he should've been angry at the possibility of losing everything he knew and loved, but that was not the primary emotion that rose to the surface. As he looked into Morgan's wide brown eyes, he felt sympathy for what she must be going through. He could rebuild his life at The Stables. He had family and friends who cared about him. But she was completely alone in the world. All because she wanted to do the right thing and put some criminal in jail.

They were alike in that way, both of them trying to do the right thing. He was beginning to understand why she had been so secretive with him. Her true identity coming out could have ended her life. The anger he'd felt earlier had subsided. "If Jesus can die on a cross for the likes of me, I can forgive you for all that I've been through."

Morgan gazed at him, unable to answer as some unnamed emotion played across her features.

The woman came into the living room holding two bowls. "I thought you two might be hungry. It's nothing fancy, just some oatmeal with banana slices."

Alex felt as though he'd been handed a steak-and-lobster dinner. He hadn't eaten for at least sixteen hours.

They ate quickly. When they walked through the kitchen to return the bowls and thank the young mother, a second child, a girl of about five, had joined her sibling at the table.

"I appreciate your kindness so much," said Morgan.

The woman took the bowls. "You're welcome. I think it's what any Christian would do, don't you?"

"Yes," said Morgan, visibly shaken by what the woman had said. "That's so true."

They walked outside to the back of the house and across the field. Up ahead, he could see a road. "What that woman said upset you."

Morgan stalked across the field. "It didn't upset me. It struck me that there are kind people everywhere. People who love God and try to do the right thing even if their safety is at risk. I've seen the worst of humanity. It's nice to be reminded of the other side."

"All because of a bowl of oatmeal," Alex said.

"Yes." She stopped and turned to face him.

"And because of you." Her eyes glowed with affection. "Knowing you has been a faith builder."

Her compliment was bittersweet because he knew in a few hours he might never see her again. "Glad it made a difference, Morgan."

They waited for only a few minutes before a dust cloud stirred up by a car coming toward them became visible.

Alex tensed as he peered out the barn door. He drew closer to Morgan. He needed to make sure this wasn't another ambush. He wasn't taking any chances.

"That's it. That's the car Serena said they'd be driving."

They came to a stop and a tall man and dark-haired woman got out of the car and ran toward them. Morgan hugged the woman.

The man turned toward Alex. "Sir, you're going to need to come with us."

Alex complied. He and Morgan got into the backseat. They drove through the countryside. Alex wondered what his fate would be. Could he go back to his old life, or would he become a prisoner like Morgan?

Gradually, the countryside disappeared, the houses grew closer together and Morgan could see the Des Moines skyline in the distance. Tension knotted the back of her neck as she thought about the uncertainty she faced.

Alex had fallen silent beside her in the backseat. Had he grown weary of the price he had to pay to be with her, to do the right thing? She knew with certainty that all he had done for her showed that he loved her. What did it matter, though? They couldn't be together.

Morgan stared at the back of Serena and Josh's heads. The events of the past twenty hours raged through her brain.

"Did Deputy O'Toole..." She couldn't bring herself to say it.

Serena glanced at Josh and then turned to face Morgan. "He's in pretty serious condition, but they think he'll make it."

The news may as well have been a sword through her heart. He had been seriously hurt trying to protect her.

"The local police did pick up one of the men you described—the man in the baseball hat." Serena turned back toward the front of the car and continued to talk. "The FBI interrogated him all night. He's a local thug hired by Josef Flores to make your death look like an accident."

Morgan sat back in her seat. Considering

Deputy O'Toole's grave injury, capturing Beige Cap felt like a bitter victory.

She remembered what Josef had said about knowing that a plan had been made to move her. She leaned forward in the seat and spoke to Serena. "Josef knew that I had put in a request to be moved hours after I did it."

Josh responded from the driver's seat. "That's suspicious. We're starting to think there must be a leak in our office."

Serena nodded. "How else could he get that information so fast? Plus we think someone in the office suppressed information that should have gotten to us sooner."

Morgan leaned forward in her seat. "What are you talking about?"

"We had an FBI guy look into your car accident more closely. That drunk driver never got anywhere near the road you were run off of," Serena said.

"The agent filed the report, but it never got to us." Josh's voice filled with anger.

Serena turned to face Morgan. "If that information had gotten to us sooner, we would have pulled you out faster."

Josh and Serena proceeded to talk about the leak and what it meant in the front seat. Their voices faded when Alex leaned toward

Morgan. "You were going to leave The Stables the day we went to the baseball game?"

She nodded. "Not that day. It would take a while to get things set up and I wanted time to say goodbye."

"So you were going to leave, just like that." She saw hurt in his eyes.

"I was afraid I was going to share everything with you because I..." She had to say it. "I wanted you to know who I really was because I'd fallen in love with you."

Warmth pooled in his eyes, and he reached up to touch her cheek.

They neared a large brick building in downtown Des Moines. Josh pulled to the curb, then turned around and faced Alex. "This is where you'll go for questioning. An agent will come out in a moment and escort you inside."

Panic seized Morgan's heart. "You mean we're being separated?"

Serena made a phone call. A few seconds later, an older man in a dark suit pushed through the door and stalked toward them.

Serena turned so she could face Morgan. "We need to get you to a safe house as quickly as possible. We can't risk you being out in the open."

The man waited on the sidewalk while

Alex pushed open the door. The look in his eyes made her want to fall into his arms. Would she ever see him again?

He shut the door with one more glance in her direction as the car edged back out onto the street.

"You'll stay at the safe house until we can get your new identity in place," Josh said. "First, we'll need your help with some things related to this case."

Morgan leaned back in the seat, giving in to the sorrow that swept over her. That was it then. They'd set her down somewhere in the world with a new name…alone.

"What's going to happen to Alex?"

"The FBI needs to find out how much he knows about your case," Josh said. "He was aware that you were in the Witness Security Program, I assume?"

"Yes, he figured it out." She stared out at the passing buildings.

They drove away from downtown toward a residential neighborhood where the houses were far apart. They slowed, and Serena hit the garage door opener and eased the car into the attached garage of a classic suburban home.

Morgan pushed the door open while Josh and Serena waited for her. They stepped into a house that could exist anywhere in America—wood floor, granite countertops and neutral paint colors. The only thing that indicated this was a safe house was the drawn blinds. Morgan plopped down on the couch.

"Are you hungry?" Serena asked.

"I guess I should eat." She didn't feel very hungry, though. Heartbreak over parting with Alex had zapped her appetite.

Josh and Serena spoke in hushed tones in the kitchen and then Josh entered the living room. "We need to talk to you about something."

It took her a moment to pull herself free of the sadness about Alex. She could feel her anxiety increase as Josh craned his neck to see how much longer Serena was going to be with the food. Then he turned back toward her. "You're a hot target right now."

"What does that mean?"

Serena came and sat on the couch a few feet from Josh. She placed a sandwich on a plate on the coffee table between them. "It means that right now the people behind this adoption ring are actively looking for you."

"Josef Flores is probably still looking for you," Josh said. "If we can take him in, we can question him, find out who he's working for."

Morgan had a feeling where all this was leading. "So you want me to be bait."

"A sting would serve two purposes. In addition to catching Flores and whoever is helping him, it would give us a chance to confirm that there is a leak. We will control the information so it doesn't get outside of the St. Louis office. If Flores shows up, we will know someone in the department has been feeding him information."

Serena leaned forward and touched Morgan's knee. "The choice is yours. We're asking a lot of you."

She didn't need to think about it. Although she knew there were other men behind all this, she would sleep better knowing that Josef was behind bars. "Of course I'll do it." This would not end unless she stepped up. And she would never be able to stop looking over her shoulder until all the people involved were caught.

"The narrative that will be leaked is that you were brought in, but that you gave us the slip, a believable scenario. It happens with witnesses who are tired of the rigid requirements of the program. The morning of the sting, word will go out that you've been spotted jogging in Gray's Lake Park."

Morgan absorbed what she had been told.

"So Josef and maybe even the men who were helping him will be caught?"

Serena nodded.

Josh rose to his feet. "We'll work out the details over the next twenty-four hours. In the meantime, Serena will stay with you at the safe house."

Serena stood and followed Josh to the door. They spoke in whispers for a while longer.

Morgan picked up her sandwich. All of this felt so abrupt. She had told Alex her true feelings too late. She pressed a pillow against her stomach and lay down on the couch as sadness washed over her.

The FBI agent sitting across from Alex tapped his pen on the table and flipped through the three pages in front of him.

It had been five minutes since Alex was led into this interview room and the agent had only asked him his name before reviewing the report. The silence only served to reinforce the sense of loss he felt. Morgan was gone. He'd never see her again…and she loved him.

The agent was an older man with steel gray hair and knobby hands. He had a habit of pursing and unpursing his lips while he thought things through. He cleared his throat. "For the record, this interview will be recorded."

"I understand," said Alex.

"How do you know Morgan Smith?"

"She came to work for me at the horse stable I manage."

"You had no contact with her prior to that?"

Alex shook his head. "No."

"When did you become aware that she was part of the Witness Security Program?

"A day ago. Though I'd suspected it before that."

"And did she divulge that information to you?"

"After I guessed it," Alex said.

"What specifically did she say to you?"

"That her real name was Magdalena."

The agent shifted in his chair. "Did she give you a last name?"

"No."

"Did she explain to you why she was in the program?"

"She said that she was a witness to a crime. That she hadn't committed any crime."

"Was she specific about the case she was a witness in?"

Alex shook his head.

"Please give a verbal answer."

Alex leaned forward. "No, she didn't share any details."

The older agent stared at him for a long

moment. "Do you intend to get in touch with or seek Morgan Smith out anytime in the future?"

The question pierced his conscience. The agent was trying to figure out if there was a risk of his compromising Morgan's new identity. But the question meant something entirely different to Alex. "I'd like to," he said.

The agent drew his bushy eyebrows together. "Excuse me?"

"I'd like to see her again."

The agent shuffled his papers. "That would be highly irregular."

Alex took in a breath. "I really need to see her again." He was having a hard time picturing his life without her, and she had said she loved him.

Seemingly flustered, the agent tapped his fingers on the table. "This is not a situation I've ever encountered in all my years at the bureau."

"Please, can you pass the message on to her?"

"I can, but it's up to her."

Alex nodded. There was the possibility that she would say no. "I can accept that."

NINETEEN

Serena sat across from Morgan, holding a file on her lap. A cell phone rested on top of the file. "Do you remember you told me when you were in the hospital about a Dylan McIntyre who processed the paperwork for the international adoptions on the American side of things?"

Morgan nodded.

"We've tracked him down. He's a lawyer who works for a St Louis law firm." She set the phone on the coffee table and pushed it toward Morgan. "We need you to call him. We have to make sure we have the right Dylan McIntyre. Do you think you'd remember his voice if you heard it?"

Morgan's anxiety level rose with each question that Serena asked. *Focus on the big picture, Morgan.* This was about Baby C and Baby Kay and all the other children. "Yes, we had a pretty long conversation. That's why I remembered him at all. So I just need to identify him as the Dylan that I spoke to?"

Serena shook her head. "We don't know if he's involved or not. He's our next link in the chain. I need you to talk to him. Tell him what you know about the children being taken. I'll be listening in to gauge his reaction." Serena opened the file and pulled out a piece of paper that had a phone number and a list of questions written on it. "This is his work phone number. Make the conversation seem natural, but here are some possibilities for questions you can ask that might clue us in about how much he knows about the illegal adoptions."

After looking over the questions, Morgan took a breath, said a prayer and dialed the number. Dylan picked up on the first ring.

"Hell-o." Morgan gripped the phone a little tighter.

"Yes, who is this?"

"I don't know if you remember me. My name is Magdalena Chavez. I was the American who worked for an adoption agency in Mexico. We talked a couple of times." Her throat had gone completely dry.

"Oh, yes. How are things going at your end? I haven't heard from you folks in months," Dylan said.

"Dylan, I have something to tell you. I have

reason to believe that the agency I worked for was coercing and blackmailing mothers to give up their children, and they might have kidnapped some babies, too."

There was a long, heavy silence on the other end of the line. Serena made a whirling motion with her hands that meant to keep him talking.

"The agency in Mexico closed. Weren't you told that?"

"Nobody told me." His voice was tinged with anger. "I assumed you had a slowdown in the adoptions or had taken your business elsewhere."

Serena pointed to one of the questions on the page.

Morgan read where Serena pointed. "You processed a lot of adoptions for us. Didn't it strike you as strange at how quickly the adoptions went through?"

"What are you saying?"

Morgan was afraid Dylan might hang up as she got closer and closer to accusing him of illegal activity. "Most international adoptions take years. How long were your adoptions taking?"

Again, there was a pause before he responded, as though he were absorbing the full impact of what she had told him. "The turnover was much faster than that. Look, I know where you're heading with this, and as far as I know, these adoptions were legitimate. I would never participate in something as heinous as what you are suggesting. I have children of my own. I only want to protect children." As he spoke, his voice grew louder and more intense.

"The babies were being taken over the border and given to the parents. That's a violation of Mexican law. Did you know that?"

"I'm just the guy who handled the paperwork." Dylan sounded extremely upset. "You'll have to excuse me. I will look into this." The line went dead.

Morgan set the phone back on the coffee table. "What did you think?"

"I'm not sure." Serena bit her lower lip and focused on a distant object. "Sometimes when people are guilty, they protest overly loudly."

"I was used as a way to lend the agency in Mexico legitimacy. Maybe the same is true of Dylan," Morgan said.

"Or he was fully aware of what was going on. We'll see," said Serena, still lost in thought.

Serena's phone rang. She rose to her feet and wandered away from Morgan, who listened to the one-sided conversation.

"That's outside of anything I've ever dealt with. The guy has certainly proven he was on Morgan's side." She glanced over at Morgan. "Okay, I'll ask her." Serena pulled the phone away from her ear.

She turned to face Morgan. "It seems that Alex Reardon wants to see you one more time."

Morgan tried to process what this meant.

Serena nodded as a faint smile emerged.

Morgan felt a mixture of joy and confusion. Would this only make their goodbye harder? "I guess that would be okay." She did want to see him, even if it was the last time.

"Okay, I'll let them know." Serena got back on the phone and wrapped up the conversation.

Morgan was still in shock. After all she had put him through, after everything he'd lost because of her, he still wanted to see her.

Serena moved into the kitchen and set the kettle on the stove. "This guy must really care about you."

Morgan rose to her feet and paced. She crossed her arms and stared at a landscape painting on the wall until it went out of focus. The kettle whistled. A minute later, Serena handed her a steaming mug of tea. "He must love you tremendously to agree to go through all this."

Morgan took the mug. "He's been through a lot already." And still, he wanted to be with her. He'd proved his love for her over and over. She wouldn't push him away ever again even if it was just one last time.

Alex could feel his anticipation growing as he was driven through the city streets. The thought of seeing Morgan, of holding her in his arms, sent a charge of joy straight through him. He didn't know the man who had picked him up, but he had identified himself as a U.S. Marshal. He had agreed to wear a blindfold so he couldn't identify the location of the safe house.

What kind of crime could Morgan have witnessed to have this high level of security? The car turned a tight corner and came to a stop. He heard the sound of the garage door opening and then the car rolled forward.

"Okay, take the blindfold off." The marshal pointed toward a door. "Go on inside there."

Alex pulled the blindfold off and stepped out of the car as his excitement grew. He pushed open the door, walked down a hallway and entered the living room, where Morgan sat with her head bent, looking over a map with Josh and Serena.

She raised her head, a smile lighting her face as she stepped toward him. He held out his arms, and she fell against his chest. He kissed the top of her head.

Serena cleared her throat. "I think we should step out for a minute."

Josh nodded. They disappeared through a side door.

Alex placed his finger on her chin and tilted her head. Her eyes filled with pure love for him. His lips brushed over hers. Her hand touched his neck and trailed over his ear as he drew her closer and deepened the kiss. After several more kisses, she pulled back and looked into his eyes again. "I'm so glad to see you."

"Me, too. Really glad." The words were bittersweet. In a few hours, she might be on a plane and his life would have a hollow ring to it.

Josh and Serena returned.

"Morgan, we can finalize the plans and then you and Alex can have some time alone," Josh said.

Serena addressed Alex. "We're almost done. This won't take more than twenty minutes."

"Plan for what?" Alex cut his gaze toward

Morgan. That veiled look fell across her face. What was going on here?

Serena stepped in. "Alex, Morgan has agreed to be part of a sting operation to catch the men who came after you two."

He wrapped his arms around Morgan's shoulders. "That makes her a target." Anger colored his voice. How could they do this to her after all she'd gone through?

"It was my choice." Morgan's voice was steady, unwavering. "It has to be done to end all of this."

His anger dialed down a notch. He understood her logic. Morgan wouldn't have a normal life until the people who wanted to hurt her were in jail. "Then I'm going with you." He drew Morgan close and gazed down at her. Josh and Serena gave each other a look.

"Give us a moment," said Josh. They stepped into a corner, their heads close together as they talked.

"I have to do this," said Morgan. "Otherwise, this will never end and more babies will be harmed."

He didn't know what she meant by babies being harmed, but he had a feeling he'd know soon enough. "Then we'll do it together." He squeezed her shoulder.

She gushed, "Why would you do all this for me?"

"Because I love you, silly. How many times and how many ways do I have to show it before it sinks in?"

Josh walked over to them. "The extra protection for Morgan would be good. After what you two went through on your own, Alex has proven he can hold his own."

Serena added, "Morgan told me everything you did when the two of you had to run from Josef. I don't think she'd be here if it wasn't for you."

"Let's get you up to speed." Josh stepped over to the coffee table. He grabbed the map and pointed out where marshals would be positioned. "Once she goes over this bridge, there's an area that is very secluded. We think that is where Josef is most likely to be waiting. You have to let Morgan go there alone. Make some excuse—that you pulled a hamstring, that you have something in your shoe, whatever. We'll all be close, ready to jump, but she has to look vulnerable."

The tone of Josh's voice revealed the level of danger this operation involved. Alex would do anything to ensure Morgan's safety. So much could happen in that moment when she was exposed.

"Both of you will be wired so we can communicate with you," Serena added.

The four of them ate a meal together and reviewed the plan several times. Alex alternated between studying the map and talking with Morgan through the evening. She told him about Mexico and the baby-snatching ring and all she had been through up to this point. The more they talked, the more he saw that maybe they could build a life together when this was all over. He only hoped they got that opportunity.

TWENTY

The morning was overcast with an on and off drizzle as Alex pulled into the parking lot that bordered the park.

Morgan sat in the passenger seat, her stomach tied in knots. The only thing that lessened her fear was having Alex close.

A car that she knew had two marshals in it pulled into the lot a few minutes later. The other marshals were already in place along the trail.

Alex turned to face her. "You ready for our jog?"

She nodded. If he was feeling any fear, he certainly wasn't showing it. They pushed open the doors.

Alex gathered her into his arms and held her. His warmth surrounded her, giving her strength. His heart beat against her ear as she rested her head on his chest. If only this moment could last forever.

He pulled away and kissed her gently. "Let's do this."

Morgan looked into his eyes. "Okay."

They headed toward the jogging trail. She kept the pace slow, not wanting to expend too much energy. Morgan glanced around. The weather had kept most people away. A few people walked their dogs, and she saw joggers and bicyclists on the trail up ahead. They rounded a corner and entered an area of the park that was heavily wooded. Morgan slowed down even more. She could see the bridge up ahead.

The sound of Alex's feet pounding behind her stopped. She gazed over her shoulder; he had stopped and was leaning over with his hands on his knees. He offered her a nod. The expression on his face was probably designed to assure her that everything was going to be okay.

Morgan jogged over the bridge and slowed to a stop. She studied the thick trees around her. A marshal was supposed to be stationed somewhere around here. She did a calf stretch and watched the perimeter. She continued to stretch, tuned in to the sounds around her.

All she heard was the drizzle of rain on leaves. As she leaned to touch her toes, her heartbeat drummed in her ears. Despite the coolness of the morning, she was sweating. How long should she wait here?

She stretched a few minutes more and then she heard Serena's voice in her ear. "He might be a no-show. Why don't you get moving? Walk, don't jog."

When Morgan looked over her shoulder, she couldn't see Alex. What kind of order had he been given? She walked, glancing side to side. She heard noise behind her, a bicyclist moving at a high speed.

"On your left," said the bicyclist.

Morgan moved to the right edge of the trail. Tire wheels whizzed. The blow to her head was so sudden she barely comprehended that it had come from the passing bicyclist. She saw a whir of color and heard the wheels spinning away and fading as she fell to the ground. Hands hooked under her arms and dragged her into the trees. The last image she saw before everything went black was of Josef Flores sneering at her.

As he had been ordered, Alex jogged over the bridge. He spoke into his mike. "She's not here."

Serena's voice vibrated in his ear. "Keep jogging. She hasn't come into view of the next marshal."

He slowed his pace. Up ahead, a bicyclist sped down the trail and disappeared around a corner. Alex took in his surroundings. He was only yards from where the next marshal was stationed and still no sign of Morgan. He quelled the rising panic with a deep breath.

You're no good to her if you fall apart.

He focused on what he needed to do, not on what might have happened to her.

"Her wire's been cut off." Serena's voice held a note of anxiety. "We're moving in."

Alex scanned the area. She must have been hauled into the trees. He searched one side of the trail, which led back to the more crowded part of the park. He dove into the other side, scanning side to side as he zigzagged through the trees. The trees thinned to a lake where rowboats could be rented. A man was pushing a boat toward the water. He recognized him as the one Morgan had called Josef. Morgan could be passed out in the boat…or dead. Josef must be planning on dumping her in the lake.

Alex raced up to them, catching Josef off guard. Josef reached into his coat for a gun. Alex hit Josef across the jaw and the gun went flying.

He could see Morgan in the boat, looking lifeless and pale.

Dear God, don't let her be dead already.

Josef lunged at him, his hands prepared to wrap around his neck. Alex dodged him and landed a blow to his back and then another to his head. The larger man went down to the ground.

Morgan's boat had drifted farther away from shore.

Alex spoke into the mike that fed to the marshals. "I've got Josef. He's on the shore by the boat rental."

Josh's voice came through loud and clear. "We're on our way."

"I need to save Morgan." The tremble in his voice gave away his fear. What if he hadn't found her in time?

Alex scooped up the gun, shoved it in his waistband and swam toward her. His muscular arms sliced through the cold water, but the weight of his clothes slowed him down.

He grabbed the rim of the boat and pulled himself in. He saw Josef begin to stir on the shoreline. He leaned over Morgan. All the color was drained from her face and her lips had turned blue. His heart seized. He placed a hand on her cold cheek. Water from his hair dripped onto her face. "Morgan?"

Her eyes fluttered open and relief spread through him.

Focus came back into Morgan's eyes. "You're soaking wet."

"I know. Let's get you to a safe place." He grabbed the oar and rowed toward the shore opposite Josef. Josh and another marshal showed up on the shoreline and handcuffed Josef, who was still trying to recover from Alex's attack.

Alex stepped out of the boat into the water and pushed it the remaining distance to shore. He held out a hand for Morgan to take.

Serena was waiting for them on the opposite shore. She ran toward them. "Come on, we've got to get you guys out of here. We've got Josef, but the other man is still at large."

"The guy on the bicycle," said Morgan.

"Let's go." Serena, who was usually cool under pressure, had a lilt to her voice that gave away that even she was concerned at this point.

She led them through the trails out toward the parking lot.

Alex crawled into the backseat with Morgan and wrapped his arms around her. He kissed her forehead. "We're almost home, baby."

Serena wove through traffic. "I've got a tail."

Trying not to panic, Morgan craned her

neck. There were two lanes of traffic, so she couldn't figure out who was following them.

"The white compact car about three cars back?" Alex asked.

Serena turned down a side street. "That's the one."

After twenty minutes of quick right turns and weaving through residential neighborhoods, Serena parallel parked the car. She tapped her fingers on the steering wheel. She checked her mirrors several times and then got out and searched the trunk. She returned with a blanket. "I know you need to get out of those wet clothes, but this should help keep you warm."

Alex spread the blanket over both of them and held Morgan close. Eventually, his shivering subsided.

Serena made several phone calls, the gist of which was that they were being taken to a different safe house. They drove out of the city and through the day until late afternoon. This safe house was much like the other one, just a house in another subdivision in another city.

After parking in the garage, Serena rested an arm on the seat back. "Josh should be waiting for us inside."

Morgan had barely had time to process everything that had happened. As the adrenaline wore off, fatigue set in. "I'm glad they caught Josef. I hope it helps in some way."

"You made a huge difference. Josef Flores is no longer a factor. We clearly have a leak in the department and Dylan McIntyre is a strong lead. Also, we know Baby C's mom's name was Vanessa."

Alex held her tighter. He whispered in her ear, "I'm so proud of you."

Serena looked at Morgan. "We'll stay here with you tonight and then we'll bring a marshal to stay with you for a few weeks until we can set you up with your new identity." Serena pushed open the car door. "Alex, we can arrange for transport for you back to The Stables."

Serena's words sent a panic through Morgan. So this was goodbye. They had put it off as long as they could.

Alex turned to face Morgan, his eyes filled with love. "I don't want to go back to The Stables. I want to stay with Morgan."

Morgan's heart fluttered when he gazed at her.

"We only relocate spouses and children with the one in witness protection," said Serena.

Alex never took his eyes off of Morgan. "That's exactly what I'm saying." He gathered Morgan's hands in his. "Morgan, will you marry me?"

She couldn't believe what she was hearing. Of course it was what she wanted. "Yes, Alex, I'll marry you."

"If they can, do you want one of the marshals to marry us right away?"

Even though she was weary, cold and hungry, joy burst through her. "Oh, Alex, that sounds like a wonderful idea."

He kissed her.

Ten minutes later, she found herself searching the closet in one of the bedrooms that contained a sparse amount of clothes in various sizes. She found a light blue dress with crochet on the hem and sleeves. Not much of a wedding dress, but it would do.

She heard a tapping at the door, then Serena came in holding a bouquet of tulips and daffodils. "From the yard. I know it's not much."

She took the colorful bouquet. "They're beautiful."

When Morgan stepped into the living room, Josh was waiting, holding a Bible. Alex had changed, too. It looked like he had found a pair of jeans that fit, but his shirt was a plaid short-sleeve done in shades of green and pink.

As she stood beside him, his smile warmed

up the whole room. She touched his rather loud shirt. "It's a story to tell our grandchildren, right?"

Alex smiled and they both turned to face Josh.

"When the paperwork goes through, you'll be married under your new identities. You understand that, right?"

They both nodded.

Josh opened the Bible and spoke. "The four of us are gathered here to witness the sacred rite of marriage before God..."

TWENTY-ONE

As he surveyed the busy airport, Alex grew anxious. Morgan had gone to get something to drink more than twenty minutes ago. They needed to get to their gate. Josh had given him the information about their new identities, but Alex had kept their destination a secret from Morgan. He wanted to surprise her with where they were being relocated. The marshals were waiting for them at the gate.

He turned a half circle, scanning the sea of faces. What if something had happened to her? He walked toward where she'd pointed when she said she was going to get a drink. He rounded the corner and still didn't see her. Tension threaded through his chest.

This couldn't be happening. She wasn't at the coffee shop or anywhere else. Had they been followed to the airport and now the thugs had nabbed Morgan?

Alex turned again and hundreds of faces raced past him, none of them Morgan's.

"Hey, there!" Morgan's voice was like a symphony to his ear.

He whirled around. "There you are." She didn't need to know he'd almost lost it. "Where did you go?"

She smiled slyly. "We didn't have rings for our wedding, so—" She pulled a box out of a bag. "I got us some." She flipped open the box. "It's nothing fancy, just airport jewelry."

"Another story for our grandchildren."

"We'll have to modify it, of course, leaving out the part about witness protection."

He took the simple silver band and put it on his finger. "Mrs. Waverly, I think that's a great idea."

They'd chosen the name from the horse sale when he'd first felt that spark of attraction. Chipper's Boy and Bluebell just didn't work as last names.

"Thank you, Mr. Waverly. Now, are you going to tell me where we are going?"

He pulled the tickets from his pocket. "Seattle, Washington."

Her face lit up. "Seattle? Sounds like a great place to start a new life."

"Anywhere you are is a great place to be."

He looped his arm through hers. “Don’t you think?”

“I do think so, Mr. Waverly.”

He led her toward the gate to board the plane and step into their new life.

* * * * *

Dear Reader,

Morgan faces much adversity, loneliness and danger to help the U.S. Marshals close in on the mastermind behind the illegal adoption ring. In addition, she has had to sacrifice a great deal. One of the things that helps Morgan persist in her mission is the reminder that what she is doing is a small part of a bigger mission. Because the crimes being committed happen in many cities and even internationally, it will take diligent work on the part of Josh and Serena to make sure the people responsible are put behind bars.

Though I have never had to do something as difficult as Morgan had to do, I have often felt discouraged about persevering as a parent or continuing church volunteer work. I see just one small piece of the big picture. It is easy to get overwhelmed by the struggle, to wonder if my choices are making a difference. It is a nice reminder to me that God sees the big picture, how my choices to persist against adversity connect with other people's choices. That is where trust comes in. Whether it is helping a teenager work through their anger or holding a crying baby in the church nursery, I have to trust that doing the right thing, however small, is part of God's larger plan and that good things will result.

Sincerely,

Sharon Dunn

Questions for Discussion

1. What happened to Morgan in Mexico?
2. How has it affected her faith?
3. Why does Alex have trust issues where women are concerned? Do you think he is justified in feeling that way?
4. What does Morgan do that makes her seem untrustworthy?
5. When he came to manage The Stables, Alex made a dramatic job change. Why did he work at his old job, and why did he make the change?
6. Have you ever switched jobs to pursue your life's calling?
7. Morgan must live cut off from her past and from her family. Do you think you could do that?
8. Why does Morgan believe Craig is a good person despite his actions?
9. What does she do to cause Craig's heart

to change? When do you clearly see that change?

10. What things happen to Morgan that makes her think her identity has been compromised?

11. What was the most exciting scene for you?

12. Both Morgan and Alex like to ride the horses as a form of therapy. Do you have something you do that is better than talking to a counselor?

13. Who was your favorite character? Why?

14. What helps Morgan regain her faith?

15. To be with Morgan, what does Alex have to give up? Would you do something like that for someone you loved?